A SEA OF DEAD

by Robert Fowler

Any references to locations, people, organizations, establishments and events are fictitious and intended to only give an aura of authenticity. This book is a work of fiction only.

Dialogue, characters and incidents are all taken from the author's imagination and are in no way portrayed as real life events.

All Rights Reserved. No part of this publication may be reproduced in any form or by any means, including scanning, photocopying, or otherwise without prior written permission of the copyright holder.

Copyright © 2013 Robert Fowler

Author Robert Fowler

Published by New Net Media

Cover Art by Ed Norden

ISBN: 9781493780372

http://AuthorRobertFowler.com

https://www.facebook.com/AuthorRobertFowler

OTHER BOOKS BY ROBERT FOWLER

LAST BUS HOME

Like a snippet of a conversation possibly overheard on the last bus home this short story by Robert fowler introduces us to Scott Williams with no background, and no fanfare as he meets a girl from the other side of the tracks called Jet, while up town shopping for a book one evening after school.
The story concentrates on the random meeting of these two polar opposite teenagers, and the simple yet excellently written story and the realistic dialogue move you swiftly through an exciting and somewhat bizarre encounter in young Scott's life.
As with all good short stories I wish it had been longer and would have loved to have known how things ultimately played out for the two teenagers, though as a longer story it may well have lost some of its bite. All in all one of the best short stories I've read in a while, very good job Mr Fowler

SWALLOWS AND ICE CREAM

This is such a well written book that pulls on the heart strings. Easy to read but left such an impact

I thoroughly enjoyed reading Swallows And Ice Cream. The author really brings you in to the story and brings the characters alive. Steve is riddled with guilt over his beloved

Kathryn, he is young and tormented and the enticement of beautiful young Maria cannot suffice. I found this book to be a gripping story of love and passion but with an unexpected twist.

ACKNOWLEDGEMENT

Yet again, I would like to thank Tania Parsons from New Net Media and Joolz, for all their hard work, support and dedication.

Leon Slater and Michelle Sharman, for again being my sound board.

To my family for their kindness, support and loyalty; standing by me through thick and thin.

With the Autumn leaves falling and the night's drawing in, longing for yet those long Summer days.

DEDICATION

In respect to the fallen; for their courage and dedication.

A SEA OF DEAD

PROLOGUE

Captain David Sherman has been sent to recover from injuries received in the trenches of France.

It is 1918, and the war is already over for some like David. Scared and invalided, he will have to begin a new life. He is staying at the house of Lady Almina, who has opened her house and grounds to help with the war effort. There David meets Marlin Walker, an attractive widower who helps around the estate.

The captain is captivated by Marlin, to him she is unlike any woman he has ever met, but that is where his problems begin. As well as his physical injuries, he also suffers from endless nightmares and a deep feeling of guilt that he has returned alive, when so many did not.

Much more of a complication, is the fact that he is also married with two daughters, and his father-in-law is a rich and powerful businessman; David's obsession with Marlin sets off a chain of events that could lead to his downfall.

A SEA OF DEAD

APRIL 1918.

    My finger travelled across the uneven surface of my jawline, the hot jagged piece of metal had entered to the left of my chin, and dug a trench along for several inches, before emerging from the flesh nearer my ear. I stared at the mess that was now the lower part of my face; the reddish raw dead skin that overlapped in layers, where no vegetation would grow ever again, unless I allowed it to grow like a tramp may have done, only then would the wound be hidden from prying eyes.

    It was as I did this that she swept into my life like a sandstorm in the desert, without warning, from nothing to a deluge and all done in calm silence. Her presence filled the room and I became merely its guest and not its occupier; my eyes wandered back to the mirror and to the laceration, and all at once I felt repulsed and had to avert my eyes once more.

    Was it her beauty which suddenly highlighted my new ugliness? Or had I not really looked hard enough at

A SEA OF DEAD

my newly constructed appearance? Either way I felt the need to keep the left side of my face away from her scrutiny. She set about my unmade bed; the untidiness of my room was like a boil on clear young skin; my eyes surveyed the room and I saw for the first time, the empty bottles, overflowing ashtrays, scattered books and soiled clothing, along with the filthy glasses and plates that cluttered this pigsty.

She moved swiftly around the room as if floating on fresh air. The swish of her dress was the only sound that resonated in the room. Moment by moment my living space began to resemble what it had looked like when I first entered it almost five weeks ago, yet she held no magic wand; not having seen her before, I wondered if she only attended lost causes.

Now at the mahogany table by my bed, she rearranged the small clock so it could now be read, not that I had any need of it; time had stood still for me here. It was as she dusted the photo of my wife and two children that I felt a tremor run through me; I did not want her to look at it, or touch it, but the minute she began to dust the glass surface, I wanted to scream at her to put it down, instead I remained silent.

'Will you need any help with bathing?' Finally she spoke in a sweet soft voice, matching her eye-catching looks.

'I've washed already,' I answered.
She moved to the window. 'A little fresh air will help I feel.'

A SEA OF DEAD

It was only as the first waft of fresh morning air filled the room, that I realised how stuffy and stale it was in here. I had been seated all the while, however I felt I should stand; immediately the pain in my leg exploded and pulsated setting my muscles on fire.

'You're new?' I asked.

'No.'

I reached for my cigarettes but stopped; it would mean contaminating the room which now smelt fresh and almost clean.

'I haven't seen you before.... was what I meant.' I added.

She glided a cloth across the windowsill; it collected an unhealthy amount of dust and I felt ashamed at that moment, although it was not my responsibility; I was here to rest and recover after serving King and Country.

'I work on the estate... and have done so since I was thirteen years old.' She spoke as she moved her duster across the tiny shelf adjacent to the window.

I tried to guess her age but she had a face that gave nothing away; thirty perhaps? No more than a year or so either way nevertheless. As yet she had not smiled, unlike the nurses who did so at the drop of a hat; like a soldier salutes an officer, it was required of them.

'What do you do?'

'Clean up pigsties as well as other things.'

I smiled and looked away embarrassed, yet nevertheless I felt instantly at ease with her.

'I do laundry, help in the kitchen... whatever needs doing really, my mother worked here before me and when she died...'

'I'm sorry,' I broke in.

'Don't be; it was ten years ago now.'

'Still...' I stopped but decided to say no more. She continued to busy herself around the room, going into the small wardrobe and hanging up whatever had fallen, which seemed to be the entire contents. I wanted her to stop and sit for a while, maybe to talk, but mostly so I could look at her; I also wanted to know more about her.

'Well that's all I can do for now,' she said straightening her dress. 'I'll leave you to have a pleasant day captain.'

'David.'

She looked at me; it was the first time we had stared into each other's eyes. Hers were a clear watery grey like two tiny lakes, that on a hot day would entice you to plunge in headfirst; today was not sunny, neither was it hot, but I would have immersed myself in them that very minute.

'Don't go,' I said without thinking and waited for the consequence of my request.

She said nothing. Instead she gave me a look of curiosity, before leaving the room. I still felt her presence long after she had gone.

◈

A SEA OF DEAD

It was good to feel the mild breeze sweeping about my face and through my hair; it forced me to close my eyes. The sound of a thousand tiny leaves high up in the trees caught my ear; it appeared to sound like a comforting lullaby to those who strolled beneath. The sky was a mixture of white, grey and blue patches that met here and there, getting on like old friends before separating and going their own way.

That was when I saw her for the second time; it was as I reopened my eyes for the umpteenth time; she was pushing a wheelchair and talking to its occupant, smiling like she had not done in my company. Immediately and without reason I felt jealous; why him? I thought; because of his injuries? Could that be the reason? I suddenly realised how immature I was being, and immediately felt ashamed.

She passed twenty yards from me, her conversation still ongoing but undetectable to my ears. She looked up and in my direction and for a second time that day our eyes met. I was certain her look was one of surprise, like someone trying to recall a face.

I removed a cigarette from my silver cigarette case and tapped it several times on the lid, before placing it between my lips. Not once did I take my eyes from her. She was now busy tucking a blanket around the poor wretch, her smile warm and radiant, he himself was young and handsome. He smiled back at her and they laughed about something one of them had said; I felt envious of his looks, and what seemed a too intimate relationship with her. They set off again and I saw her look back in my direction, I was certain her lips had formed a weakened smile.

※

    I had found a wooden bench which overlooked where the hills and fields overlapped each other. Bushes and stone walls divided green and beige fields, cottages with smoke emerging from chimneys sat nestled amongst groups of trees. It was a comforting sight; England, home, although it was not mine it was the nearest thing to it. The landscape had a comforting effect on those here trying to come to terms with the war, what they had witnessed, and what they needed to forget.

    I had not been home in over seven months; five had been spent in France fighting, another month in a field hospital after my injury, and more than three weeks spent mainly in bed here, in an attempt to recover both my strength and my mind. At first I had yearned for home, yet now somehow I felt I did not belong there anymore.

    From nowhere a gentle breeze kissed my cheeks; it would be dark in a couple of hours, but I decided to remain outside in the fresh air. But it had stirred a memory; my mouth progressively became dry, and I had to suck in the air around me, my chest became tight, and inside a panic built up like a fire gaining momentum. I felt a sickness rise to my throat.

Sweat formed on my forehead and neck, and my shirt stuck to my skin; I felt lightheaded, and began taking long deep breaths, filling my lungs before allowing it to leave from my mouth. I leaned my head back and felt a chill wash over my body making me shiver.

I saw flashes of light and felt the ground move with a sudden violent jolt; tiny clumps of mud began to fall back to earth. I looked down and saw my feet submerged in a watery brown substance, and placed the whistle in my mouth but did not blow it. In my right hand I held my gun which was still attached to the string that looped around my neck.

'Captain Sherman sir,' I heard a youthful Scottish voice close to my ear. 'Captain Sherman...' He spoke again.

'What?' I leant towards him.
Bursts of light were all around us turning night to day; smoke and explosions intermingled yet all those around me seemed calm as they waited for instructions; only Private Young seemed unable to wait.

'On my whistle Young... not before.' I tapped my watch with the barrel of my revolver.
On the other side of me a boy suddenly threw up, he rested his helmeted head against the side of the trench and I rubbed his back. Private Young still had one foot on the ladder, I saw the way he looked up and it worried me;

he showed no sign of alarm or panic, it was as if he could not wait, while the rest of us remained terrified of what was to come.

'Sir,' he shouted.

'Stand steady.' I said and looked at my watch; my eyes strained to see its face; down here I could use a lighter, but instead I waited for the light of another flare to slice open the night sky, and it came almost instantly; I looked again; two minutes.

I turned and faced the wall of mud, allowing the gun to hang while I undone my trouser buttons. I leaned my face against the damp earth and let the smell of the soil drift up my nostrils, it reminded me of decay, I could taste it upon my lips; as my tongue swept across them, I tasted death.

I emptied my bladder and felt the relief, just for a second I was at ease with the world. I looked around whilst doing my trousers up and saw Young looking at me again; he was waiting with the rest of them for me to send them all to their deaths. I sucked in a mouthful of air and placed the whistle between my teeth; there was no need to look at my watch, and I would blow when the next flash lit up the sky.

For a split second I was blinded, I blew but heard nothing. Young moved swiftly up the ladder as the boy who had been sick collapsed to the ground; a wet stain growing around his groin. I looked back up at Young who was almost at the top of the ladder, when he reached it he suddenly stopped, taking up his pose just like he had said he wanted to do. He looked down at me smiling, I smiled back as his head exploded, and for a split second he remained calmly looking at me.

I reached down and took hold of the collapsed soldier's collar; he looked up at me and I saw a boy, seventeen or eighteen I could not tell; I lifted him onto the bottom rung.

'GET YOURSELF UP THAT FUCKING LADDER BOY.' I screamed.

With eyes full of fear and moist from crying, he began to climb each wooden rung one at a time. The bombs exploded and the bullets whizzed around; the sky continued to be set alight and now it was my turn to climb the ladder and ascend into hell.

I climbed with purpose, not to get to the king's enemy but to ask the dead a question. I blew again and again on my whistle urging men on, encouraging them: boys, husbands and fathers to sacrifice their lives; the war to end all wars, a war we needed to win to save... to save *what*? I could not think what it was that was worth saving.

I found myself standing over Young; I stopped blowing the bloody whistle, he needed to hear what I was about to say. '*Why* Young...? *WHY DID YOU DO IT?*' He said nothing; his eyes stared at the constant flashes of light in the sky. I wished I had my pencil with me now to capture the smell of fear and the look of terror; the revulsion of war in its entire splendour. This horror needed to be shown to those who slept in their comfy beds back across the channel.

Another flare lit up no man's land, and there, ten feet in front of me, lay what was left of the boy; he would not walk into heaven *that* much I knew. He stared at the sky too; his face seemed to be asking a question that nobody on this battlefield could answer.

The biggest flash of all almost blinded me. Before I felt something caress my face, the feeling that something was tearing at my uniform overwhelmed me. I wanted to push it away, shake it off as if being attacked by an irritating wasp on a summer's day. I staggered back and raised my gun. *'OFF ME,'* I shouted and began to fire into the air. I heard Young laughing, and even the boy turned his head to look at me; I stopped and smiled back before a black cloud descended upon me.

I felt myself falling to one side, certain that I had screamed out loud; I hoped I had not, for I reserved my screaming for the isolation of my room. My throat was so dry and I felt a pain behind my eyes as if something behind was trying to force its way out. I became disoriented the more I tried to wake myself; the world seemed intent on moving in an anticlockwise way.

'Are you okay?' I heard a voice ask. Somehow the voice acted like a calming hand resting on my shoulder; it began to soothe me.

My head then rolled to one side before falling forward, the world had again moved without any prior warning.

A SEA OF DEAD

'Breathe in deeply,' the voice said.
I did not question it, but began to follow the instruction until I started to feel that my feet were, indeed, touching the ground.

'Good... again... good...' The voice continued to talk me through my demise; now I felt a hand in the middle of my back slowly begin to make circles. I wanted to close my eyes and just let the hand continue to do its work.

'Keep breathing.' said the voice.

Finally I leaned back against the slats on the bench; blindly I took out a cigarette and lit it, blowing a cloud of smoke out into the darkness. I loosened my tie and took another long draw. It was her again sitting next to me; suddenly she stood.

'Where are you going?' I asked.

'To get a wheelchair.'

'I don't need a bloody wheelchair... please sit down for a moment.'

'I am not one of your men captain, may I remind you.'
But she did sit down.

'Sorry... I didn't mean to sound so rude, or for that matter to seem so ungrateful.'

'But you did... And you were.' She was quick to reply.

'Will you accept my apologies?'

She sat back and I looked into that face again, at her cheeks which were softly rounded before they fell away like the hills that surrounded the estate. I had an urge to trace my finger down the side of her face, down to her chin and then to follow the line of her neck downward.

'How do you feel now?' she asked.

'Give me ten minutes could you? But no wheelchair please, I'll make it back under my own steam.'

'Have you something against wheelchairs captain?'

'No.'

'Then why not use one?'

'No.'

'Would you like me to walk you back?'

'That would be nice.'

'Okay but if you fall as I think you will, you won't mind if I just leave you there and go home, where I should have been twenty minutes ago... Pride,' she whispered as she stopped speaking.

'What?' I asked.

'The thing that causes men to do stupid things.' I shook my head but said nothing.

'Is it that feeling of helplessness?'

'No.' I said abruptly.

'Okay are you ready to go? I would like to get home tonight captain.'

I stood and immediately felt the urge to sit back down again. She extended her arm but I felt loath to take it; *'pride'* I said to myself. I took a step then another; she seemed so self-assured, I took strength from that. The hills and landscape below were now shrouded in a dark cloak. My head began to whirl, I closed my eyes but that just made it worse. *'Shit,'* I allowed the word to slip from between my lips; I took a deep breath and tried to slow the world around me down again.

My legs began to feel that they may give way at any moment; I smiled at her out of sheer panic, and saw a glimpse of one in return.

'You're doing well,' she whispered.
With that I felt the strength re-enter my legs; I suddenly remembered I did not know her name, but right now I needed all my concentration to get myself back to the house. Step by step I moved towards the great house, my shoes now wet with the early evening dew; the closer I got the weaker I became.

I stumbled and felt myself fall forward, I saw the ground rise to meet me, and closed my eyes waiting for the impact when a rigid arm came across my chest; I gripped it with both hands, hoping it would remain steadfast; to my delight it did just that.

'Captain we are nearly there... Take a deep breath again... Hold on to me and compose yourself... I've got you.'
The smell of lavender filled my nostrils; sweet and soothing, I began to breathe her in, gulp after gulp I drank her down.

'Do you feel alright to go on?'

A SEA OF DEAD

She had placed her other arm in the small of my back, I wanted to say *'no'* but instead I smiled at her; I felt both her arms tighten. *'Slowly,'* she whispered and I began to move each foot one after the other.

I could find no way of recovering my strength, I felt angry with myself. *'Not now,'* I said under my breath, *'please not now.'* I looked up; the house was less than thirty yards away, surely I had it in me to make that short distance, but it was evident that it was going to be a futile attempt. My knees began to buckle; I had no control over my legs. I heard a voice shout from the direction of the house.

'Marlin... do you need a chair?'
As I stood wobbling on my legs, I repeated in my head over and over, *Marlin... Marlin... Marlin.*

'Marlin,' I said aloud.
'Yes.'
'Marlin.'
'Sit.'
Where? I thought, the bench was no longer there, we had left it back in the darkness.

'Sit captain.' I was told again.
I felt my body being lowered slowly; down and down I went, I looked up and saw several faces, none of which I recognised, *'alright,'* her voice came from behind me, and all at once my backside touched a firm surface.

'Thank you lads,' was about the last thing I heard. I was drifting towards a dark sea, gliding across the water

making no ripples or sound; I felt she was still near to me, I could still smell lavender; I was safe.

※

'Apparently you gave them quite a scare David.' The woman's voice echoed around my head; my mind sifted through countless faces trying to place it to one of them.

'If it was not for that nurse... well not a nurse it seems, they would have found you lying on the grass... God knows what would have happened to you... you have to be more careful.'

I saw the shadow of my wife move across the wall, the lamp burned by my bed and I could sense it was dark outside. I stayed silent, I had neither the strength nor the inclination to join in this one-sided conversation; I heard a cupboard drawer slide open, wood upon wood like a roar that never grew louder; I remained mute.

'Sometimes I feel you do it all on purpose... like a child needing attention.'

I wanted to sleep, for her to go away, to stop talking, her words were one continuous row of letters, one after the other, making no sense to anyone who listened to her. She alone was the only person to decipher what she was saying.

A SEA OF DEAD

I longed for Marlin, for her to come and rescue me. I had remembered her name and that pleased me; there was a knock at the door.

'I sent for a nightcap darling.' She spoke whilst opening the door.

I heard the hinges creak and the rattle of china; could it be Marlin? I suddenly thought, and felt the need now to open my eyes.

'Ah there you are David.'

I saw Mary standing next to a nurse in a dark blue uniform; it was not her and I had blown my cover.

'David... let's sit you up... I have some cocoa for you... and a tea for me.'

I dug my elbows into the mattress and with every ounce of strength left in me, pushed myself upright.

'Hold on.'

Mary slid a pillow behind me. 'Thanks,' I said, trying to catch my breath like a man twice my age. I lowered myself down and looked into her blue eyes.

'How do you feel David?' she asked with as much concern as she could muster.

She hated this place, her father had offered to have me moved to a private hospital near where they lived, as ill as I was then, I made my point that I wanted to be where other soldiers were, and I wanted to be with my fellow comrades.

'Fine,' I mumbled.

'You do not look it; they can't be feeding you properly... I told...'

'The food's fine Mary... the place is fine... like you said I overdid it, stayed out too long, I thought I was stronger than I was; it won't happen again.'

'They should not have let it happen in the first place David...'

'Don't blame them... I'm a big boy now, I go and fight in wars and get blown up...'

'No need David to...'
She reached for her handkerchief and held it to her nose; it reminded me of her mother.

'When they told me you had collapsed... I... I...'
She burst into tears.

'I'm fine now... really... I just need some rest, a good night's sleep.'

'You have been sleeping for over a day now,' she said through sobs, 'and you look no better.'
She was standing over me now and I could feel her breath on my face, I smiled up at her, unable to understand this exaggerated display of concern.

'Trudy and Elizabeth are at the hotel in the village.' She wiped her eyes. 'I wanted them to see you, but I'm glad I didn't bring them tonight, I would not want them to see you like this.'

'I won't look any better tomorrow.'

'I don't mean your face David... it's how unwell you look.' There was a small glimpse of anger from her.

'I know what you mean.'
It made me smile to think of my girls; little Lizzie as I called her was eight, all blonde curls, with a mischievous

look on her face, while Trudy now almost eleven, to my unease, was already being turned into a woman by Mary and her mother.

'Are they well?' I asked.

'Yes, both are back in the room making you get well cards.'

I smiled.

I remembered the first time they saw my face, I was terrified that they would scream and rush away, I could not have been more wrong. Both crept up to me while I lay there, first Trudy touched the wound, then very carefully Lizzie did the same.

'Does it hurt?' they both asked.

'No, but my leg does.'

'But we can't see your leg papa.'

A child's mind; what can't be seen can't affect you. They spent the rest of that evening touching my jaw at intervals, like they were visiting the zoo and I was one of the animals.

But I was glad that Mary did not bring the girls every time, the corridors and grounds were teeming with injured men; mainly amputees with their missing limbs, but even those hardened to war winced when confronted by men that looked like they came from a nightmare.

Captain Lambert, in the room next to mine lived in a dark world without mirrors or visitors except his surgeon and a nurse. One side of his face was missing, blown to pieces by a grenade; he wore a grey cloth over his face which covered almost all of it; I had the

A SEA OF DEAD

misfortune of sitting next to him while he ate a chicken stew; he found it hard to swallow, so loaded his spoon before positioning it at the back of his throat, the noise was repulsive and yet I felt sorry for him, because he would never know the gentle touch of a woman, or the joy of companionship, he will never return to civilian life. But there were plenty of other poor wretches who walked about the grounds with their faces scarred beyond recognition. Some wore tin masks, others had their faces swathed in bandages with almost nothing of their features showing, and what remained uncovered, looked as though it should have been hanging in a butcher's window, this too I found alarming.

     Mary spoke about home, her father whose business building slums in the south of England was thriving and about the future; more precisely, my future. I sat thinking about Marlin; I had no interest in *'daddy's business'*, in fact I had not thought about what was going to happen to me when I left here.

I would have to leave the army, that much was obvious, but then what? Strangely the future did not worry me in the slightest, there was a time when it would have, yet here I was married, with two children and thinking irresponsibly, and to cap it all thinking about another woman. I smiled to myself before noticing Mary glaring at me.

'You're not listening to a word I'm saying David.'

     'Yes I am,' I lied, 'I'm just tired... sorry.'

'No it's me who should apologise... it's just not seeing y...' She turned her head away and moved her hand towards her face.

I found it hard to recognise Mary through this deluge of rare affection towards me.

'I'm sorry Mary.' I leaned forward and placed a hand on her arm, not the act of a man in love, but more of friendship, both admitting guilt to be polite, yet neither opening their eyes to the reality of their dilemma. Intimacy had long since vanished from our relationship, that act had produced two lovely children; nothing more could be gained by passing bodily fluids, the reward had already been secured.

Mary came and stood next to where I lay, she lowered herself so that I could kiss her cheek; I saw where her tears had run just moments before, and part of me felt a gloom descend, there was something tragic about it. Where had it all gone? The laughter, the passion, the love, or had there been any love? I found myself searching my memory; for some unexplained reason I needed to know there had been some love, if not, what had it all been for?

※

I had been confined to bed for three days; each time the door opened I felt a surge of anticipation that it could be Marlin, but instead a nurse in a blue cotton chambray dress with its white apron and red cross would enter and smile asking me how I was, and I would reply *'very good thank you nurse,'* and smile back at her.

I played a game to relieve the boredom; I invented a past for Marlin. Age twenty nine, unmarried and untouched; instead she had given this house and the lady who owned it her complete loyalty. She did not know the feel of a kiss, or the touch of a man's hand upon her body, she had decided long ago to wait for the right man, however long that took; I smiled content with my work as I slipped into a daytime nap.

'How are you feeling?'
My mind had been hovering between forty winks and dead to the world, so it took a moment to register her voice; in an instant I was awake and staring up at her face.

'Fine...' I mumbled before smiling. 'Won't you sit?' I continued.
She hesitated a moment, but then to my delight she sat on the bed. She placed her hands together on her lap and I found myself staring at her like some lovesick schoolboy.

'So you feel better today?' she asked.
'I felt better yesterday... but it seems they needed reassuring.'
'Maybe you don't fill them with confidence Captain Sherman.'
'David.'
She looked at me and I saw her lips move slightly apart, unable for a moment to construct a reply.

A SEA OF DEAD

'I don't know you well enough... captain.'
I had no answer, instead I imagined myself kissing those lips, placing a hand on hers, feeling her smooth soft skin, but in the middle of my fantasy, reality crept in unseen to destroy that moment of bliss. I saw my jaw in all its ugliness, even now, in my imagination, I saw myself pull away from her face unable to pollute her beauty.

I looked away and wanted her to do the same.

'You have some colour at last.' From the open window her voice mingled with birdsong and the rustling of trees; I felt the breeze enter the room, saw the loose hair which hung like a curtain above her eyes move ever so gently, and I envied its inconspicuous presence. To touch her unnoticed was a fanciful notion, because if she could not see me but just feel my touch, then maybe I would stand a chance of removing the obstacle, my ugliness.

'Do you live around here?' I asked.

'I live on the grounds; a small cottage I shared with my husband.'

The word *'husband'* had the same effect upon me as those German shells which constantly fell about my ears, making the earth beneath my feet tremble and vibrating up through my body, making me hold my breath until the danger passed.

'Are you well captain?' she asked suddenly.

It seemed I had gone into a trance, her being married had thrown me, it was the end of my fantasy, and I felt a cold sweat form on my body.

A SEA OF DEAD

'Yes... fine... I'm fine sorry, just sometimes... well.'
She smiled but the look of concern remained on her face, and that pleased me. 'Go on,' I said. 'Tell me about him.'

'He worked at the stables, right up until his call-up. I worked for Lady Almina in the main house.'

'How did you come to be here?'

'My mother brought me here when I was just thirteen, my father had vanished when I was six; I don't remember him at all. She worked in the kitchen and the main house doing various jobs. I just did whatever I was asked to do, I picked it up by trial and error, but they were good to me and Lady Almina took a liking to me.' Marlin stood and walked over to the window and gazed out of it.

'My mother died when I was nineteen years old after a short illness, her ladyship was very good to her; it was Lady Almina's own doctor that attended to her, but there was nothing they could do.' Her eyes stared into the distance as if searching for something, I knew the view well, the valley falling away from the house; I wanted to get up and stand next to her, so we could look together.

'How old were you when you met him?' I asked.

'Alan...?' Her eyes seemed to widen. 'I was twenty four and had never had a boyfriend. After my mother died I felt so alone, I never strayed from my room except to work. My mother's sister asked me to go live with her, but I declined. I had a job here and in a strange way felt safe around the house.'

A SEA OF DEAD

'And when did you meet...?' I found I could not say his name.

'We met one day down in the village, he had seen me many times he told me later, but had been too shy to speak; if you had seen him…' A smile came across Marlin's lips, so large that I became jealous of the man it was for.

'He was such a large man, yet so gentle; he walked me home that day and the next. We sat and talked, and the hours I spent with him just seemed to pass in a flash; we fell in love, married and moved into one of the empty cottages down by the north entrance.'

'And happy ever after,' I added.

'And so we thought, but then came the war.' She almost breathed out the words, again she went silent but on this occasion she looked down and not out. 'I remember him the day he left, so smart in his uniform, so proud, so beautiful.'

I did not want to breathe at that moment, I felt like an intruder, she was no longer telling me the story, for I, as well as this room did not exist; I had no reason to disrupt what seemed total peacefulness, she was lost somewhere with him, so I looked away.

'He returned in early 1915.' She began to talk in a low voice still with her eyes fixed out the window. 'He was missing his left leg, and the lower part of his left arm. Also his left cheek and ear were mutilated.' She stopped and drew in air.

A SEA OF DEAD

Enough now I thought, I wanted to speak of pleasurable things, maybe her favourite colour, what she enjoyed doing on her days off, if she did indeed have any days off.

'Lady Almina was wonderful to us, she allowed me to nurse him every day, and she even came to visit him on several occasions. I stayed with him all day and through the night; I saw the look on the face of the doctor each time he examined him; I'm certain that they thought I was simple, I knew, I saw him every day, I felt the fight go from his body, but he did fight, he fought a brave fight and he made me proud.' A single tear travelled over her cheek.

'I understand.' I spoke in an unconvincing way, I had never met this man, yet I understood what she was trying to say; but I could not feel anything for him, instead I only felt pity for her, and the loss she had had to bear, my heart bled for her and not him. I said nothing, for if I had, I doubt I would have set eyes on her again.

I thought about all the letters I had sent back to people like Marlin, telling them how brave their husbands, brothers or sons had been. I wrote so many that they all blurred into one. I knew some, but not all the men I wrote about; I stopped grieving for them all, feeling that my letters passed on that task to others, others like Marlin, who could continue to mourn without me having to witness it at first-hand, except here I was doing just that, and it angered me; I had wanted to wash my hands

A SEA OF DEAD

of this torment and anguish, and instead I had to endure this beautiful woman's suffering.

'He died in my arms one cold February morning; we saw the sunrise together, he rested against me, I placed my hand across his heart and felt it gently fade, each last beat extinguishing life until it beat no more. We stayed like that for over an hour; the nurse found us, she smiled at me and touched my face, she was so kind, she did not try to take him from me, but instead began to tidy the room before going to fetch the doctor and her ladyship. We buried him in the village graveyard five days later.' Now she turned and looked directly at me. 'It was well attended, he was very well thought of, and Lady Almina sent a beautiful wreath... red and white...' Marlin suddenly stopped talking.

'It must have been hard for you.' I sat forward wishing I was not in this bloody bed.

'I think it must be harder to die, don't you think?'

'Yes, sorry you're right, I wasn't thinking.'

'When you love someone captain, nothing you do is troublesome or demanding, you never think of it like that. Not to be able to do anything would be the most unbearable thing I could think of, at least he was back with me, somewhere where he felt at ease, somewhere more pleasant to die, and he died in my arms and not on some stretcher in the middle of a field with a stranger looking down on him.'

I did not know that such love existed; I had never witnessed it or felt it. Once again I became resentful of a

A SEA OF DEAD

man I had never met; how had he extracted this much love from just one woman? In a passing thought I wondered if that meant she had no more to give now, I almost felt a panic inside me, a sickness that I could not remove, I wanted her to go, or I wanted to be gone myself, it all seemed too much for me to bear, as selfish as that sounded to my own ears.

She turned to face me and tried to place a smile on her lips, her hand wiped away the remnants of tears; so sad yet so beautiful. How was I to win this gorgeous creature now? I was no match for this dead man; he had far too many noteworthy attributes that I had no way of competing with.

'The doctor spoke to her ladyship, and said how well I had done looking after Alan, so after a short period away at my aunts, I returned and helped both in the kitchen and with the men.'

'Did you not want to become a nurse?' I asked.

'That's a calling... no, I would help until the war ended, then I did not want to witness anymore suffering brought about by governments which sit miles away and never see the misery they cause.'

'I think you would make a good nurse,' I said, 'you have something soothing about you, like the other night when I wasn't too well, just your presence was enough, I don't know what it is but you have it.'
She smiled now. 'Well...' She began to move towards the door. 'Maybe you'll tell me when you know what it is I have.'

A SEA OF DEAD

'Don't go.'
'I must.'
'Why?'
'I have things to do captain.'
'Let someone else do them.'
She gave a gentle laugh. 'Would you like me to get someone to get you a wheelchair, so you can sit in the garden?'
'Only... if you come as well.'
'Sorry captain, but as I said I am busy, but no doubt we will meet again.'
'When?'
'You are demanding captain...' She lifted her head and looked back out of the window. 'And you'll find that putting demands on my time, will not always achieve the result you require.'
I leaned back into my soft pillow. 'I'm sorry, it's just that I like...'
'And will you please stop saying you're sorry; it's another thing I find annoying about men, if you have to keep saying it, then you must be doing something wrong time after time, meaning that you're not learning from your mistakes.'
I smiled in the hope of drawing one from her, wanting to remove the harshness from her face.
'I will see you when I see you... I'm afraid I am not one of your men... you cannot command me.' She turned to walk out of the door, but stopped and looked

back at me. 'I cannot believe I spoke as I did just now captain, I will have to be more careful about what I say.'

'You can tell me anything.' I said.

'That's what worries me captain.'

∽ॐจ

    I hardly slept for thinking about her, I went over all the foolish things I had said, and how her straight talking had made such an impression upon me. There was an inner strength about her I admired; unlike most women she did not dwell on her misfortunes, although I could see the pain was still very raw.

    But I also found her sexually arousing, there was something seductive in the way she held herself, upright, she moved with grace, but also with purpose. Her breasts were small and rounded, firm looking; her eyes teased you to come closer. A woman who knew her own mind, she had whetted my appetite like no other woman had ever done.

    My eyes searched her out as I sat in the grounds a day or so later, now I was restored to some reasonable health. My heart leapt for joy on several occasions, only for it to be deflated when I had been mistaken. I went over and over the conversations I had had with her and then added the questions I wished to ask I even anticipated the answers. I hoped on next seeing her she

A SEA OF DEAD

would view me as a good friend, or maybe a lover; my mind began to race away from me.

I decided to grow a beard to hide the revolting disfigurement; I could do nothing about the lip, or the way I leaned to one side when I walked, like a ship listing to one side in deep water. I placed a folded piece of paper in the heel of my left shoe, and paced my room hour after hour in an attempt to straighten myself. I walked towards the full length mirror, I made a pathetic sight. Was this how she saw me as well?

It was two more days before our paths crossed. With the aid of a cane I walked in the grounds one afternoon, as always my eyes explored my surroundings in case she came into view. I stopped and lit up a cigarette; I sucked the smoke into my lungs, it was then I heard two people laughing, one I assumed was a young boy.

He sat inside a wooden wheelchair being pushed by Marlin. He had a beaming smile on a young face; he could not have been more than nineteen, a product of a rich family I assumed for one so young; his cheeks were a rosy red, and he had curly jet black hair. She looked up and across towards me and our eyes met; I dipped my head acknowledgingly.

The boy twisted his body around, looked up at her then over to me it was at that moment I saw the extent of his injuries. He had both legs missing from just above the knee, his right arm had been removed from the shoulder, and his right ear seemed to be missing. He was a pitiful sight for someone so young, the smile on his face seemed misplaced, and I wondered what on earth he had to smile about.

Marlin began to tuck the blanket around the boy, whilst doing so her dress caught in the wheel, she moved the chair forward in an effort to free it, but instead it became that much more entangled.

'There's nothing for it, you'll have to either sit on my lap, or remove your dress.' The boy chuckled.
I arrived as the boy finished making his request.

'You're a cheeky monkey Tommy Gilbert; what your body's missing you make up for with impudence... if I did remove my dress... the moment you saw my ankles you would cry for your mummy.'
They both began to laugh and I had to clear my throat for them to acknowledge my arrival.

'Ah our knight in shining armour,' said Marlin as our eyes met.

'I don't want to be rescued... tell him to go away.'

'How ungrateful you are Tommy, the captain here has struggled to our aid.'

'Well tell him to limp off somewhere else.'
For a split second I thought about giving him a piece of my mind but managed to hold my tongue. The moment he said the word *'limp'* a picture of me walking came into my mind and with it all my confidence flooded out, making me feel of no consequence. I bent down and removed her dress from the spokes; I wanted to remain

on my knees, unable to look either of them in the eye, but finally I rose and stood level with her.

'Thank you brave knight,' she said with a smile. I went to speak but the boy was too quick or I was too slow. 'Okay let's go.' He almost shouted it.

'Not so fast Tommy; thank you again captain, today it was your turn to come to *my* aid.'

'I'm glad I could return the favour.'

'Enough... come on,' said the boy.

'I will leave you here if you persist in being so rude Tommy.'

I wanted to cheer, the boy was a pain in the arse, legs or no legs, and I found it hard to find any pity *in* me for this young rascal.

'Maybe we could have tea together later?' I spoke without thinking, putting the boy further into his place.

'She can't,' he said. 'She's bathing me tonight, isn't that right Marlin... tell him.'

'I'm afraid he's right captain, but even if I was not, I would not have taken you up on your offer.'

'Why not?' I asked.

'You have a wife to keep you company.'

'She's not here.'

'Any port in a storm captain.' And with that she began to push the chair.

The boy swivelled around and gave me a smirk, which led to me not defending myself against her accusation, instead I felt resentful and envious of the boy as I watched her pushing him. I felt angry with myself, but also more in love with the woman than ever.

※※

Elizabeth dangled her legs off the bed, while Trudy sat with her mother; we had all hugged and the girls had asked a thousand questions. At times we had all spoken at once, not one of us listening to the other. Mary sat looking content with life, and why not? She had everything; healthy children, a rich father and a husband who did not have to go back to war, that she could now keep and manipulate to her heart's content.

'Father has paid for the roof to be made watertight David.'

'Has he?'

'But mother wants you to come and stay with her and father when you are allowed to leave here.'

The thought would be enough to slide me back into the jaws of death. It was like a game of tennis, she hit the ball over the net and I hit it back, it had been like that for the past five years, without these small rallies there would be nothing but silence between us.

And now the separate beds, soon, like mummy and daddy, separate rooms. I looked at Trudy, already so like her mother, so clean, so sparkly, never a hair out of place, and similarly, hardly ever a smile on her face. Then Lizzy, chocolate around her mouth and in her hair;

A SEA OF DEAD

a mischievous look firmly fixed to her face, and always doing something to upset her grandparents, something which always made me smile, drawing long daggered looks from Mary.

Mary had sent the children down with her mother, which meant that she wanted to talk to me.

'Have they said how much longer you have to stay here David?'

'I have a meeting Wednesday, I might know more then.'

'I hope so, the children are becoming restless, the journey makes them irritable, and we could all do with some normality back in our lives.'

'Don't you think I want that too Mary? Nothing's been normal for the past four years and I understand how you feel, but if you had been where I have, and seen what I've seen, then you would know how much I want what you call normality.'

Just then the door opened and in walked Marlin.

She stood for a moment holding a jug of water; Mary turned to face her.

'I've come to change your water,' she said.

I sat rigid and my heart beat at twice its normal rate, I looked at Mary and wished she had not been there. Marlin came and replaced the empty jug next to my bed; I smelt her lavender fragrance and I breathed it in. Still with the old jug in her hand Marlin bent down and picked up a nightshirt I had discarded, I closed my eyes with embarrassment.

A SEA OF DEAD

'I'll take this down to the laundry room,' Marlin whispered.

It was a strange feeling, Marlin holding my nightshirt in the same room as my wife, there was something sensuous about both being in the room at the same time. Mary had once been sexually attractive to me, but familiarity had eroded any passion that remained, to the point where neither of us bothered with the physical side of our marriage.

Marlin on the other hand was sexually arousing, yet what was more gratifying was how you wanted to be in her company, that seductiveness she had about her was balanced with a breathtaking persona. She had qualities I had never seen in a woman before, a vulnerability matched with a hidden strength, kindness wrapped around a strong sense of honesty that would wound any person who took her to be a fool.

'No... No need.' I reached out to take back the nightshirt.

'David let the woman do her job,' said Mary. Marlin turned to Mary and a weak smile slowly formed on her lips.

'She's not the cleaning woman Mary.'

'Is she not?' Mary sat upright, looking with confusion at Marlin.

'No she helps around the place.' I looked up at Marlin and felt my mouth go dry. 'She works for Lady Almina whose house this is.'

'How nice for you,' said Mary patronisingly.

A SEA OF DEAD

'Look it's no problem let me take it,' said Marlin again.
I wanted her to leave it, I saw how Mary viewed her as the hired help, I felt it was my job to protect her, except deep down I knew she did not need my help in any way. But somehow I remembered what she had called me the other day; *'her knight in shining armour'*, and although I knew it was merely a play on words, I still felt protective towards her.

Marlin moved to the door and Mary coughed. 'I think I have a chill coming,' whispered Mary with a handkerchief pressed to her nose. Marlin lingered for a moment at the door; before opening it, she turned her head and bid us *'good evening'* then closed it behind her; I felt a frostiness fill the room, all the warmth had departed with her.

'Seems a nice woman,' Mary observed once the door had closed.

'Yes she is.'

'You know her well?'

'Not really... a little.'

'Best not get too attached... I'm told they fall for the uniform or the rank.'
I looked at Mary and my face must have betrayed my thoughts.

'Please darling, she's an attractive woman, take away the cheap clothing and you could have a seductive woman, one who could...'

'Enough.' I raised my hand. 'You don't know anything about her.'

Mary smiled. 'Have I touched a nerve David?'

'No don't be stupid, I'm just wondering why you seemed to have taken a dislike to her.'

'Your defence of her is a little robust... I thought...'

'I'm not defending anyone; it just seems for some reason and without knowing all the facts...'

'And what facts are they?'

I stopped what I was about to say, it would do more harm than good to begin to explain about her husband's death and her work here; I was not about to open up another can of worms so I yawned and pressed my head into the pillow behind it.

'Are you tired darling?' Mary enquired lighting a cigarette.

I nodded.

'Before I go you did not answer me David.'

'About what?'

'Staying at mummy's when you get out of here, so you can recover in peace.'

'Can't I think about it later?' I asked.

She walked around the bed and lowered her head to kiss my cheek, like you would a child before turning off his lamp to go to sleep.

'Yes of course... but I don't know what you have to think about, daddy said he would pay for a nurse to

A SEA OF DEAD

come and stay with us, sometimes darling I wonder what is going through that head of yours.'

I wanted her to go, her voice was beginning to grate on me, I wanted to scream at her to leave, but instead I smiled and said nothing.

'Now I'll be back Friday David, mother's coming again, and I might bring the children, I'm not sure, it would be so lovely if we could go out for tea instead of sitting in these gloomy surroundings, would you like that?' She put on her gloves. 'It's just the children, if only we had somewhere to leave them for an hour or so... oh well let me think about it.' She smiled and squeezed my hand.

She walked to the door, stopped and looked back at me.

'You are feeling better David?'

'Yes,' I replied.

'It's just that...'

'What?'

'Nothing.' She put on a false smile before turning and leaving the room and me.

I closed my eyes and began to drift, the door opened again and Marlin stood at the end of my bed. She wore a long black strapless dress leaving her shoulders bare. Her hair was swept back and from each ear hung a large round gold earring; it gave her the look of a hot-blooded gypsy. Her lips had a red gloss to them; she now moved closer to me.

A SEA OF DEAD

It was as if she was gliding on air, each movement full of grace. She stopped and looked down at me. Sweat formed on my forehead, and I felt myself become aroused. Gently she lowered her head down; her lips drew ever closer, stopping moments before they came together with mine. I could feel her breath on my face, and the sound of her heartbeat pulsated almost in a rhythm.

As our lips met and I closed my eyes, her tongue pushed its way into my mouth and I accepted it with pleasure. We kissed for a minute before she withdrew her head; I saw the smile on her lips and returned it. I moved my hand up towards her breasts and touched them over the material of her dress, they felt so firm, it drew a deep breath from my lungs; she was like a goddess and I had become bewitched by her beauty.

Still smiling, she then looked across to the door, my hand left her breasts and now my eyes followed hers. There he was laughing, Private Young with half of his head missing, laughing like a demented child. I wanted to scream, before noticing Marlin walking towards him, I looked to where she had stood moments earlier and the space was empty.

I tried to get out of bed but the sheets and blankets seemed to weigh a ton, using all the strength I possessed I could still not free myself. I looked up, now they stood side by side, he then pulled the top of her dress down over her breasts, revealing both in all their glory. He bent his head down and began to kiss them, I yelled at them but no sound left my mouth, I tried to close my eyes but could not, shaking my head I cried *'No... No... No...'* Then they both began to laugh at me and I broke down and wept, I felt the tears sliding down my face, I wanted to die like Young had and for it all to be over.

⊷⊶

    I was told to stay in bed for another day; my temperature had been high overnight after a nurse had come to check on me, although I did not feel unwell. I spent the day reading, a pointless exercise as I took nothing in. Each time my door opened I hoped it was Marlin returning my nightshirt, but it was only nurses looking in on me. When I closed my eyes I thought about the dream I had had; how real it had seemed, where even the touch of her flesh had seemed genuine.

    I could not hide the fact that I had become besotted by her, yet to think that such a woman would find me as desirable was out of the question; *her* beauty, *my* deformity, *her* charisma, *my* offensiveness; we were worlds apart, yet I would have died for her, this woman I knew so little about, but who had pierced my heart by just being there.

    She remained unaware of all this, she had never once shown any yearning towards me, I had not misread any signs because none had been sent, this was all in my head; it required no more than a look from her, or a smile, or even some harsh words; nothing on this earth could discourage or divert how I felt about her, yet deep inside I felt frightened, for I knew this would only lead to trouble and possibly destroy me.

※

On the Friday Mary arrived out of the blue with her mother in tow. I had heard nothing for the past three days, and therefore I thought nothing was happening.

'Doctor Longhorn told me I was allowed to take you out of the grounds for an hour David.' She stood with a look of triumph on her face.

'I wish you had told me,' I said before greeting her mother. 'I'm not certain I'm up to it,' I added.

'He seemed to think you are, and it will do you the world of good.'

With that she opened the doors of my modest wardrobe and began to move the hangers first one way, then another, until she pulled from it a dark grey suit.

'Here... this will do.'

Her mother ran a finger across the wooden dressing table, before holding it close to her eyes; she turned up her nose and pulled a handkerchief from her bag.

'I thought you were bringing Trudy and Lizzy to see me.'

'Yes I did.'

A SEA OF DEAD

Now unless I was mistaken, only three of us stood in my room. Mary held the suit up at the window. 'Is nothing clean in this place David?' she said. 'Mother, you better step out of the room while David dresses.'

'The children Mary?' I asked.

'All in good time David, now if you don't get a move on we'll be late for tea.'

I stood in my shirt and socks, scratching the lower part of my face; I had abandoned the idea of growing a beard for now, but that did not stop me feeling unclean. I really did not want to go out and certainly not with Mary and her mother, just the thought was enough to put me off my appetite, or what little I had of it. She did up my tie, combed my hair and treated me like a child, and *like* a child, I accepted it.

Her mother was seated outside under a large mirror, her handkerchief, as always, pressed to her mouth and nose. We walked slowly downstairs to the large tiled reception area.

'So where are the children?' I asked.

'Well you know that lovely woman…'

'What woman?'

'The one who took your nightshirt to be washed… remember?'

I went cold; where was this leading to?

'Well David, I happened to bump into her by the main gate next to the tiny cottages, and well, one thing lead to another and she said she would very much like to look after the girls, and that it would do you good to get

A SEA OF DEAD

out of the place, so you see, Trudy and Elizabeth are with your friend, safe and sound. Come on mother...'

'The smell in this place is awful Mary,' said her mother as she passed me.

I stepped outside and looked around, but there was no sign of either the girls or Marlin, instead a man stood alongside the open back door of a large black automobile. I made my way down the steps unable to fully come to terms with events; at any moment I expected to wake from this nightmare.

The car took us straight to the tea rooms, the journey there took around forty minutes. I sat and ate very little, what I did eat I found too sweet and sickly, my stomach stirred with every mouthful I swallowed. I had to ask for several glasses of water, while Mary's mother, went on and on about allowing soldiers to roam through the house and gardens in the state that some of them were in.

Mary spoke about how hard it had been to replace good men back on her father's estate with so many being called up. Some of the buildings on their estate had gone to rack and ruin; daddy had complained to the war office or someone there who was very high up that he knew, but he was told nothing could be done. I sat wondering what world they were living in; did they not know that good men were losing their lives daily? Many had nothing to come back to, no job, no home, they had had no say in it, they were not asked but *told* to go to war, most did not understand why.

A SEA OF DEAD

Mary asked again if I had thought about joining her father's business, I shook my head whilst drinking water by the gallon; my mouth became far too dry too quickly. A plate smashed on the floor somewhere behind me and my heart almost leapt from my chest; I found myself gripping the arm of my chair firmly, sweat oozing from almost every pore in my body. My heart pounded, each beat coming faster than the one before, my head spun and I began to gasp for air.

'Darling are you not well?' enquired Mary.

'I'm fine.' I tried to control the panic inside, but I felt the battle was being lost. I looked at Mary and smiled out of sheer fear; *not here* I thought to myself. It was then I thought of Marlin, wishing it was her sitting next to me, and in that moment a calmness began to descend upon me. My heart beat a little slower and my breathing became more stable.

'I feel better now,' I whispered, uncertain of whom I was reassuring.

My mother-in-law stared at me as if I had grown two heads; if I was not good enough for her daughter then, I certainly was not now.

'Should we not be getting...'
She had forgotten my name; I wanted to laugh in her face.

'David back?'

'Yes mother when he is ready.'

I sat with the window open all the way, and although it was far from cold, Mary's mother huddled

A SEA OF DEAD

herself into a ball rather like a hedgehog hibernating. She exaggerated the temperature outside. Mary, who would ignore her mother when it suited her, stared thoughtfully out through the front windscreen; I breathed in fresh air, but my body had become tense and filled with anxiety.

The car came to a halt; I looked around and for the first time noticed a row of small white cottages, set back into the fringes of a large wood. I must have been blind not to have noticed this before, but it seemed that I had missed an awful lot since arriving here.

We all stepped out of the car and began to make our way towards them. Mary's mother insisted on coming too, simply to find something more to moan about I presumed. She walked with difficulty on the uneven ground. I heard Lizzy scream with enthusiasm before I saw her running towards us, her face a picture of happiness. I smiled too and looked around for Trudy, although my body trembled with expectancy, just on seeing Marlin once again.

Both came out from the trees together; Marlin had her arm around Trudy's shoulder. She bent at the waist, so lowering herself to my daughter's height as they spoke; I'm not an emotional man but the sight of those two brought a tear to my eye. Lizzy ran into my leg and a stab of pain shot through it, but I gritted my teeth and allowed it to pass.

'Look papa...'
She held up what was left of a wild flower.
'What is it?' I asked.

A SEA OF DEAD

She shrugged her shoulders. 'I forgot.'
I lifted her with difficulty and kissed her on both cheeks. 'Have you enjoyed yourself kitten?'

'Yes and I want to come again and again... Marlin is such fun, and she let us walk in the woods, climb trees and...'

'I hope she did *not* allow that.' Mary's mother stumbled alongside us. 'Whatever next Mary?'

'I'm certain Mrs Walker would not allow any harm to come to them mother.' Mary looked first at me, before turning to face Marlin and Trudy who had reached us with large grins on their faces.

'The children were never in harm,' said Marlin.

'But look at the state of their clothes!' Mary's witch of a mother added, handkerchief in hand.

'Yes well I'm sorry about that; next time maybe you could dress them in something old or worn.' Marlin spoke as she brushed Trudy's coat down with her hand.

'These are young ladies my dear girl, ladies do not climb trees or...' Mary's mother stumbled over her words in the same way she tottered across the muddy ground, 'pick weeds... or go for walks in woods.'

'Do they not?' Marlin stared back at her.

'Did you enjoy yourself?' I shouted trying to defuse the situation.

'Yes,' both girls screamed back at me excitedly.

'There,' I turned to the old woman. 'Isn't it about being happy? Is that not what we want for our children?'

A SEA OF DEAD

Her stare told me all I needed to know about the old witch, to go and live with her would be sentencing my children to no childhood at all.

I looked up at Marlin and remembered my dream; I almost had to look away as my mind replayed part of it. I looked again at the cottages, and thought about her and Alan living here together. I envied him and wished that I too could live here with Marlin.

'You must come and see the woods daddy,' said Trudy.

'Not today Trudy,' Mary broke in. 'Daddy is tired.'

'I would like to see them,' I said looking at Marlin.
Marlin stared back at me and we seemed to hold that gaze for several seconds.

'We should be getting the children back David.' I turned to see Mary with an intent look on her face.

'Yes...' I cleared my throat. 'Yes come on girls let Marlin go and get some rest.' I looked at her again. 'And thank you again.' I added.

'Yes thank you.' Mary came over and took Marlins hand. 'Maybe my husband could pop over and you could show him around your woods.' She looked around at me and smiled. 'You would like that darling.'
I smiled and nodded my head; I was not going to play this little game of hers, not today.

Both girls ran up to Marlin with a sweet show of affection that I had never seen from them before, and suddenly Trudy was a young child again, not the transformed young lady that her mother and grandmother seemed in such a hurry to achieve. Whatever Marlin's secret was I hoped for more, I had not seen the girls this happy in a long while. It made me wonder why Marlin had not had children herself; was it by choice, or had the time not been right? She seemed such a natural mother.

Before leaving, the girls wanted some time with me, so all of us sat on the terrace. Their grandmother sat wrapped in a hideous yellow shawl, while the girls relived their time in the woods, this seemed to annoy Mary, who wanted to talk about Trudy's next school. Her father it seemed, wanted to pay for her to go to a top boarding school, something I was fully against.

And so the evening ended in a whispering row with me answering questions that the girls put to me, and Mary's mother going on and on about how cold it was getting and sending the girls to get blankets to cover her legs which were now *'like ice'* as she kept telling us. I wondered if some poor bugger lay on his bed freezing to death in one of the rooms, for she would not give a damn if that were the case.

I kissed my children goodbye and both shed tears; grandmother was already seated in the car; as Mary stood and waited for the children to depart, I knew by the look on her face the argument was far from over.

'I don't know what gets into your head sometimes David.'

'What do you mean?'

A SEA OF DEAD

'Trudy has a chance of a first class education and you want to turn it down… don't you care about your children?'

'It's because I *do*... that I don't want her to go... I want her around so I can watch her growing up, I don't want to see her every two months for ten minutes.'

'You're exaggerating; it did me no harm, and she gets to come home for one week in every six.'

'Listen to yourself, every six weeks; I want to see Trudy every night, every morning...' I turned away; I could not look at her anymore.

'They're waiting for me, but we need to talk again David.'

'Talk until you've worn me down do you mean?' Mary looked at me with her mouth agape, then turned and walked away; I stood shaking; inside I felt drained physically *and* emotionally, I needed sleep like a flower needed rain, if not I too would wither and die.

✥

I lit a cigarette and looked towards the woods, the same ones that surrounded Marlin's cottage, it had been two days since that embarrassing coming together and I had spent my time wallowing in self-pity. I had reached into the wardrobe and taken out my sketch pad, which I had hidden in the large inside pocket of my long trench coat.

A SEA OF DEAD

Mary hated me sketching, she had never once complimented me on anything I had drawn; she would make me put it away if we had visitors, or change the conversation if I unwittingly brought the subject up. So now I hid the fact that I drew, like an alcoholic sneaking a drink when no one was looking, for it seemed the act of putting pencil to paper was somehow an evil crime, something that could cause disgrace to the family.

And so I found myself walking amongst the trees in my trench coat, cane in my left hand, the leather bound pad in my right. Inside my pockets I had a never ending supply of pencils, a sharp knife for when they became blunt, a full packet of cigarettes, and to top it all, it looked like it was going to be a fine day.

I took my time; I followed a worn path and although I knew where it was leading me, I did not want to get there too quickly. I stopped and sketched a tree stump, then a view of the path ahead, before my pencil depicted several small clumps of wild flowers. They were rough sketches, for although I did not want to hurry, I also did not wish to take a too leisurely pace. My goal was to see Marlin, and I did not want to lose sight of that.

So it was an hour before I arrived at the cottages; I had filled in a whole page and had begun another. I felt relaxed for the first time in a while, although I felt a sense of anticipation run through my veins. But I worried that because she worked so many hours, she might not be there, but I could always wait. It crossed my mind that

A SEA OF DEAD

after either a long night or a busy morning the last thing she would need, was someone to turn up uninvited.

I was at the back of the cottages, so I decided to wait another twenty minutes before walking around to the front. I sat on what remained of a fallen tree and drew the cottage while I waited. I placed my cigarettes next to me along with three pencils and the knife. I felt the warmth of the sun on my back and so removed my heavy trench coat. I lit a cigarette and sharpened all three pencils and began to sketch, I was so engrossed in what I was doing, that I had not seen her coming along the path.

'That's very good captain,' she said from behind me.

I jumped with surprise, and she smiled.

'Sorry did I startle you?'

'Yes,' I said standing up to face her.

She tilted her head to one side. 'Maybe some smoke from the chimney captain, to give it that homely look.'

I looked back at the page. 'Yes,' I said, 'you're right.'

'Us woman are always right.' She smiled.

She held a wicker basket across her arm and wore a grey casual dress which hugged at her tight waist, highlighting her hourglass figure. The smallest sight of black lace showed just above her black walking shoes, which like mine were wet from the grass. She had put her hair up, although some had fallen making her look that much more attractive.

'Thank you.'

'For what?'

A SEA OF DEAD

'Your compliment,' I said.

She came closer and viewed the page again; the smell of lavender surrounded me and I breathed her in.

'Why have you hidden this talent captain... surely not vanity?'

'Nor pride either.' I added.

She smiled and I instantly felt at ease.

'Would you like to come in and have a coffee captain?'

'David.'

'Well?'

'Yes I would like that.'

Without another word she began to walk towards the cottages; I turned and picked up my coat, grabbing the pencils, cigarettes and my cane, but struggled to catch up with her. I felt a surge of excitement, an adrenalin rush of such magnitude that I had only ever experienced it before climbing into no man's land. But that had been brought on by fear; I wondered how much of this feeling was generated by trepidation. She walked through the black painted door leaving it ajar for me. Placing the basket down on a long wooden table, she went to one of the cupboards opposite.

'Five minutes captain,' she said placing a saucepan on top of a cast iron stove.

I smiled but said nothing. She walked across and took what looked like mushrooms from the basket placing them inside what I assumed, was the larder. The kitchen also served as a front room; the stairs led off to one side.

A SEA OF DEAD

A window above the kitchen sink looked out onto the woods, to where I had sat drawing just moments ago; I put my sketch pad on the large table, and looked across to where two worn leather chairs sat either side of a brick built fireplace.

In my mind I saw two happy people sitting in front of large yellow flames, both in love, and I felt my eyes begin to fill with tears, I turned my face away and looked out of the large front window whilst wiping my cheeks; I was not, it seemed, in control of my emotions when close to her.

'Are you alright captain?' I heard her say.

'Yes... yes just looking at your view this way,' I replied not wanting to turn and face her.

'Forever the artist... Always views.'

'Yes.' I smiled and relaxed a little.

Marlin moved around the place like she had in my room that first time, and although the room looked spotless, she still seemed to find something to move or wipe, eventually she placed two cups on the wooden table and sat herself down intimating for me to do the same.

'I hope you did not mind looking after my children... I had no idea she was...'
Marlin lifted her hand. 'I loved every minute.'

'It's just that my wife thinks that no one ever minds doing anything for her.'
She stopped me again. 'Let us forget that now, it was not a problem.' Marlin's lips formed a half smile, and I knew

A SEA OF DEAD

she was not going to enter into some character assassination of my wife.

I asked if I could use the toilet and was informed that it was out in the back garden. Upon my return, I suddenly felt a chill run the length of my spine as I stared at her with my sketch pad open turning over a page; now, as she looked up, I could see where something had made her eyes fill with tears.

'I'm sorry, I should have asked, it's so rude of me.'

'No... No... Please, I don't mind in the least,' I lied.

'They are wonderful captain, well drawn and yet... upsetting.' She rose from the table as I sat. 'Alan tried to describe what it was like out there, your drawings capture it completely, so when I saw those sketches you did of soldiers, I saw Alan...' She wiped a tear as it travelled down her face. 'And I saw all the horror he must have witnessed and I felt so helpless.'

I stood but did not move from the table, my mouth went dry and my mind blank, with my emotions so mixed, I did not know what to say; one half of me was delighted receiving her compliments, while it was those very same drawings that had reduced her to this.

'Please sit, ignore me.'
She smiled as she returned to her chair; I waited for her to sit before I lowered myself into the chair.

'Your children are a great credit to you and your wife,' she said picking up her coffee.

A SEA OF DEAD

'Thank you, I hope you're not saying that to be kind.'

'Captain if you knew me then you would know I say what I think. I say nothing to just please, I've offended more times than I wish to remember, but that is how I am, so people have to take me as they find me.' She smiled again at me. 'May I?' She turned the pad around to face her.

'Help yourself,' I whispered.

I was enchanted by her; I sat and stared as she looked down, taking her time on each page, studying every detail it seemed. I cringed as she turned to yet another 'war' page. During a lull in the fighting I found I could only relax by taking my sketch pad out; the men enjoyed being drawn and after they looked at themselves, they seemed to forget where they were for a short period, and that was no bad thing. All wanted me to tear out the page, but I told them that I would redraw it for them to take or send home which they all accepted. The problem was that I had no one to give these drawings to now, as all were buried beneath French soil. It was me who felt the full force of war again, and as before felt my eyes well up with tears as I remembered each man.

Silence fell on the room; I sipped my coffee as I watched her. She continued to linger on every page, as if trying to place herself inside it, so she could smell or touch what was in the drawing. Her lips formed a smile when looking at a sketch of the countryside; the men

A SEA OF DEAD

brought another look, one that made me look away from her face, away from the look of horror that I had caused.

'I never knew how powerful a pencil could be,' she whispered as she kept her eyes on the page. 'How much emotion in a person a few strokes of lead can release, you cannot just *see* the fear, but you can *feel* it as well.'

I remained silent, overwhelmed by her flattering remarks.

'Somehow part of me wishes that when I turn the next page, I will see Alan's face staring back at me, silly I know.' Then her voice faded away and I saw the tears come again into those beautiful eyes.

I found myself turning away once more, a coward to the last, unable to comfort her when she needed to be. I heard the next page turn and looked back at her, she was looking down on the drawing of a young girl seated on a straw covered floor, her legs bent with her arms clasped around her knees; she looked as I remembered her, like she had just woken.

Marlin stayed on the page, the girls large round eyes staring back up at her.

'She is beautiful,' Marlin whispered.

'Yes... yes she was.'

'Who is she?'

'A French girl; the daughter of the farmer whose farm we stayed on the night before moving to the front, which was only six miles away.'

Marlin looked up at me. 'Did you get to know her well?'

'I can't speak French.' I replied.

'I did not ask that captain.'

'No.' I murmured.

'She is young... not more than sixteen?'

'Yes.'

'Yes... younger or yes sixteen?' Marlin required an answer.

'Sixteen.' I almost whispered it. 'Your husband…' I went on.

'No captain...' She drew breath. 'Not today.'

I went to speak but no words came out.

Marlin continued to turn each page, it took another twenty minutes before she finally arrived at the last page of sketches that she had come across me doing.

'It is very lovely,' she said closing it. 'I cannot believe your wife thinks as you say she does. I would have thought these were good enough for a publisher to look at.'

'You're very kind but my wife has a low opinion of art, as does her family, she feels it should be a pastime, but no living could be made from it.'

'Really?'

'Her parents would die of embarrassment if I pursued that road.'

'Have they not seen this?' She placed a hand on the cover.

'No.'

'How strange people are.'

I shrugged my shoulders.

'So you treat this as a hobby?'

'Yes I do.'

'If I could draw like this, you would not be able to hold me back whatever anyone thought; I would want to go and capture the world for people like me who love to look at beauty and life, disturbing as it may sometimes seem.'

'Maybe I'm a coward,' I said.

'You *are* a coward captain, not in the way *you* think, but a coward nevertheless, and that disappoints me.'

At first I could not respond, she was correct when she said about speaking her mind, I regrouped as she took the cups back to the sink.

'That's a bit strong,' I said as she returned.

'Is it...? Please yourself.'

'You have to have confidence in whatever you do.'

'So do I take it I am the only person to tell you how good you are?'

'No... But...'

'No buts captain, at least give something a go, step from the shadows, what have you to lose? Doing nothing is taking the easy way out.'

I ran my fingers through my hair; I could not have imagined this conversation when I entered her cottage.

'I won't know where to start,' I said sitting back in my chair.

A SEA OF DEAD

'My Alan would never give in, he would always find a way around, under or over a problem, he would let nothing defeat him.'

'Except a German bullet...'

As soon as the words left my mouth my stomach tightened, and a sick feeling made its way towards my throat, I wished for the floor to open up and swallow me whole.

'I think it is time you left captain.'

'I'm sorry... it was not what I meant to say.'

'Captain...' She stood holding the door open. I went to apologise once more but knew by the look on her face it would be pointless. I left and my world collapsed all around me.

◈◈

For the next twenty-four hours I put myself on trial; unable to understand just why I had said what I did, and at a loss to how I was to going to get her to accept my apology, because anything I said now would sound inadequate. I woke that night dripping with sweat and wrote page after page of drivel, and now instead of searching her out, I found myself hiding away from her, praying that when the door to my room opened it would *not* be her this time.

I allowed another day to pass, but my words still sounded as brutal now as they did then. I planned to go down to the cottage and plead for her forgiveness, except I knew that what I had said would take more than the word 'sorry' to allow for my pardon. So I remained in bed another day, not bothering to shave or wash, allowing myself to slip into a state of desolation, I could think of no way back for me and so allowed gloom to set in.

    I screamed at each nurse in turn as they tried to cajole me out of bed. Each person who stepped through that door became my enemy; I left the food and just drank the water. I kept the window shut, I did not wish to hear what was going on outside, the room stunk of my body odour and finally the nurses brought the sister, who I also sent away with a flea in the ear.

I looked at my watch, it was past eleven and my appointment with Doctor Longhorn was at two, which I wanted to avoid, as I had done yesterday. I scratched at the bristles on my chin when I heard the door open.

    'Not today...' I mumbled. 'I'm not well.' I buried my head in the pillow and waited for whoever it was to go.

I heard the window next to my bed being opened. *'FOR GOD'S SAKE ARE YOU DEAF?'* I screamed. I was about to turn and face the culprit then I heard her voice.

    'How can you bear to live in this mess captain?'

    I held my breath unable to decide whether to jump for joy or hide further in my pillow.

    'That's better, some fresh air... are you going to remain there the rest of your life captain?'

A SEA OF DEAD

Finally I sat upright and ran my hand through my unkempt hair, I knew I looked a mess without having to look at myself in the mirror; two day's growth caused my face to itch. I stared at her not knowing whether I should smile; I had never felt so ashamed in my life, tears fell from my eyes and I became inconsolable.

'I'm so sorry.' I found it hard to get the words out. 'I don't know why I said what I did Marlin, but I have regretted it ever since.' She continued to bend down and pick up items left on the floor. 'I can't be bothered to do anything, shave, eat, not even sleep Marlin... I feel so bad.'

She folded another shirt and walked towards the bed; I stared at her wishing my lips could linger on hers.

'Poor you captain,' she said. 'So by doing all this…' Her eyes looked around my room. 'I will feel better? By making *yourself* feel so bad, it would force *me* to feel better and to forgive *you?*'
I stared up at her speechless.

'Is that your intention?
Again I said nothing.

'So why this childish stupidity captain…? Surely it was me you hurt! This does *nothing* to endear me to you, I see a weak man unable to face his shortcomings.'

I felt numb, like a scolded boy standing before the headmaster, I crumbled under the weight of her words.

'Marlin, please forgive me this once.'
'Why should I?'
'Because.'

'Because?'

'I'm asking you to.'

She stopped what she was doing; from outside the open window a bird whistled; I had this deep longing to be perched on the same branch at this moment.

'Do you not think that you upset me?'

'Yes I know I must have,' I replied.

'Then why is it you're lying here wanting me to take pity on you? Do you not find that strange captain? Did you not *once* think of me? Or do you only think of yourself? Did it not cross your mind that I may have been hurt?'

'I understand now,' I said.

'No... No I don't think you *do* captain, if you *did* you would not be acting the poor hard done by soul, you don't have uniqueness when it comes to feelings, it's not always about you.'

She looked about the room and I stared at her, glad that the room was now silent, because I could not take any more of her honesty.

'A beard does not suit you either captain, it makes you look old, I suggest you shave and join the human race once again.'

With that she left the room. I laid my head back on the pillow wondering if that was her way of forgiving me, I prayed it was.

A SEA OF DEAD

With my sketch pad in my hand I made my way to the cottages, I had not made up my mind what I was going to say when our paths crossed. In the army we were taught to plan ahead, not to do things on the spur of the moment, I had no plan A let alone a plan B; I would need to improvise when the time came.

I unhooked the small clasp that held the white gate shut and took a deep breath making my way up her path; I wondered if she was observing me from inside. That morning I had shaved, combed my hair and bathed. I wore a dark grey suit which I had done my best to clean up and make presentable, although I hoped she would not notice two small stains on the cuffs. It had been twenty-four hours since she had entered my room, and her words still echoed around my head. I rapped my knuckles loudly on her door and waited.

After several nervy minutes with the door unanswered, I began to make my way back towards the gate. Inside I felt a mixture of disappointment and relief, I still had no idea what I was going to say to her when confronted, yet not seeing her made me feel downcast; no amount of her disparaging words could make me feel any different towards her.

'Captain?'

I turned and saw her by the side of the cottage, with what looked like a white sheet over her arm.

'I knocked,' I said apologetically.

'I was around the back.'

A SEA OF DEAD

'Oh.'

'Come, I could use you.'

My heart leapt for joy, she had not rejected me as I assumed she would, I had crossed the first hurdle, now all I needed to do was to think before opening my mouth.

The garden was large, its boundary a mixture of thick bushes and a collapsed fence, with several trees dotted in between. A washing line went from the cottage wall, to about halfway up the garden. A mixture of tall grass and high weeds bordered an overgrown concrete path. At first glance you might think you were stepping into a dishevelled wasteland, but that was not the feeling it gave me, instead it was like stepping into another world, one far removed from your own; a peaceful, pleasant world, where *fear* would never be allowed to survive.

'Take this captain.'

She placed one end of the sheet into my hand then backed away with the other half, allowing the sheet to open out. She shouted out instructions like a first class sergeant, and I obeyed like a private. I felt strangely honoured to be asked to perform this task, done as it was in silence except for her words of guidance.

'What are you doing here?' she asked once we had finished clearing the washing line of sheets and bedding.

'I was on my way into the woods to sketch,' I lied.

A SEA OF DEAD

'So you knocked at my door?' I saw the beginnings of a faint smile form on her lips; I sensed she was playing with me.

'I thought you may want to come.' For a moment my anxiety lessened, replaced instead by boldness; I waited for a reaction.

'I'll get my coat.' She looked up towards the sky. 'Hopefully it will not rain.'

Marlin put on black ankle boots, it took her an age to do the laces up, I found it hard not to look in her direction, catching a glimpse of her calves, but I needed to remain in control of the situation, which meant not giving her the slightest excuse to convict me of any more crimes. She wore a navy blue dress which hung away from her body unlike the grey one, it buttoned up the front and I noticed she had left the top two buttons undone.

She put on a long black coat that had seen better days; the cuffs were frayed, as was the collar. There were marks here and there as well as the odd tear. She must have caught me staring.

'It's old... you're not proposing to stop for lunch are you?' She smiled.
I felt relieved; I made my smile as wide as I could, before realising how stupid I must have looked. No matter how much I tried, I could never be myself in her company, instead I seemed to jump into the bodies of people I did not recognise, trying to find the one she might like best.

A SEA OF DEAD

We walked for around twenty five minutes going deeper into the woods; Marlin seemed so at home here, completely at ease with herself. She walked without tenseness, slowly, and wrapped in a feeling of tranquillity. Every few yards she would touch the leaves on a bush, or run her open hand over blades of tall grass. She ran her fingers over the bark of a towering oak tree, as if greeting an old friend, then came to a sudden halt.

'Here,' she said.

'Here?'

'Yes it's perfect.'

I looked in the direction she was staring, to an overgrown path that cut through the wood, over it, a tunnel of green leaves. Either side were various types of trees, old stumps, wild flowers and tall bushes that seemed to explode in all directions. The trees that lined the path either stood straight or twisted and bent over to form the canopy. The path turned a sharp right before it disappeared around the corner; beyond it a small field, before the woods began again. Several rabbits raised their heads in our direction with the knowledge that they were safe in our company, Marlin smiled in their direction, and I fell deeper in love with her.

'Yes you're right,' I said as I looked up at the blue and white sky through the branches overhead. Marlin walked across and sat on one of the old tree stumps; I could now understand how the coat looked so worn, for unlike most ladies, she just sat down without worrying too much where she was sitting, it made me smile once again.

I found a raised piece of ground and made a cushion out of my trench coat, before sitting down cross-legged, but I quickly had to rearrange myself as a pain shot up my leg. I took up my pad and held my pencil poised ready to begin.

'Won't you get bored?' I asked looking up at her.

'How on earth could anyone get bored in a place like this? I'll wander around while you're working, please don't worry about me, and take your time.' She smiled a reassuring smile. 'Do you mind if I talk?'

'No,' I replied.

'Good because this place relaxes me.'

I wondered what that meant but decided not to ask. I drew a thick pencil line across the page to get my perspective and gave her one last look like a man surfacing for air before diving to the bottom of a lake. The breeze had just caught her hair and moved it ever so gently; she looked down towards the ground unaware I was watching; she looked deep in thought. It was a picture of grace and charm.

I drew in silence for the next twenty minutes, taking my time, checking and double-checking that I had got it correct. In that time I had only completed the path roughly.

'We would come walking here.'

Her voice suddenly broke the silence of the day; I did not have to ask who *'we'* were, for a moment my pencil

A SEA OF DEAD

hovered over the paper and I felt unable just for that moment to continue, anticipating more words were about to flow from her lips.

'Each evening, winter, summer, spring or autumn, we would come along this path after a long day at work. In the winter, before we set off, we would build up the fire and get a hot drink ready for our return.'
Marlin suddenly stopped and I had to look up, she seemed to be in a trance unable to continue with her recollections, I finally placed the lead onto the paper again and continued to draw; a tightness now in my stomach and a watery sheen across my eyes.

'I think we covered every inch of these woods.' Once again she took me by surprise; it had been several minutes since she had last spoken.

'People said don't you find it all the same?' She laughed. 'You could stand in the same spot in each season and it would have a different look about it, a covering of snow maybe, or drenched in sunlight, even a rain-swept day gave the view a fresh look.'

When she spoke it was as if she was speaking to someone invisible, I was certain it was not just for my ears alone.

'Alan was at his most contented here; just him and me, the world was a far off place and there was no war here.'
I looked up at her again and found her looking in my direction.

A SEA OF DEAD

'We made love sometimes... Here in the woods, against a tree or in the summer amongst the tall grass.'

The point of my pencil snapped off as I applied too much pressure; I swallowed hard; last night she was confronting me, assassinating my character, yet twenty-four hours later she was telling me the most intimate of things. I took out my knife and began to re-sharpen the end.

I continued to work with all my concentration on the page before me, yet I found there were moments when I thought about nothing but her, she overwhelmed my thoughts, and several times I had to rub out a mistake. She did wander off once, and in the twenty minutes she was gone I made up for lost time, but I wanted this to be perfect because this was for her, she was the inspiration behind it.

Almost at the end, I looked up and felt the need to capture her inside the sketch, but her consent would be needed, at which point she walked over to where I sat and stood behind me; I saw her shadow staring down at me.

'Yes... *yes* captain you have captured the *feel* as well as the visual aspect.'

'The feel?'

'Yes... each place has a feel to it, I wondered if you could catch that and I'm glad to say you have.' She smiled.

'Would you have told me if I had not?' I asked.

'Yes captain... I do not lie.'

A SEA OF DEAD

'I know,' I whispered, 'sometimes I wished you did.' She did not hear.

It was on the way back that I plucked up enough courage to ask if I could sketch her at some time. I was certain she was going to refuse outright, allowing for the time it took to answer.

'Why would you want to do that captain?'

'Because you are...' I stopped.

'Because what captain...?'

'You're beautiful.'

She turned to face me. 'Would your wife like to hear you say that to me?'

I shrugged my shoulders like a child being scolded.

'Should you not ask her to pose for you? She is very attractive.'

'But it's you I want to draw... not her.'

She stood and stared at me in silence before turning to resume her journey back to the cottage where I had hoped to be invited inside, unfortunately I found myself disappointed.

'Until we meet again captain.'

'Oh, I thought maybe a coffee.'

'Yesterday perhaps.'

'But not today?'

'No not today. Today has been too intimate, which is partly my own fault captain, but something about you makes me nervous.' She frowned. 'But

captain, a piece of advice,' she said opening the front door, 'not all women fall for compliments.'
With that she closed the door on me, leaving me holding my sketch pad, coat and cane.

It dawned on me on the walk back that she felt my intentions were not honourable, well maybe in part she was correct, but that was not totally correct. In some strange way I craved her company more than I did her body; I could not deny I found her sexually attractive, I am a man like most, driven by carnality but there had to be more to it than just sensuality, a bond that needed to be forged. With Marlin I felt I could find that, except it seemed I had given out all the wrong signals.

༺༻

Mary and her mother visited on the Sunday, we sat with Doctor Longhorn having tea and cake, and it was all very pleasant. My wife asked a million questions about my health, mainly why I could not go home sooner, to my relief Longhorn stayed resilient, *'Another fortnight'* he said with crumbs around his mouth; I made the mistake of smiling just as Mary looked in my direction.

'You seem quite content to remain here David.'

'No…' I put on a serious face. 'But surely we have to listen to the doctor Mary.'

'That was not how you saw it a few weeks ago.'

'I was ill then.'

'And you are not now?'

Longhorn lit up a cigar and blew out a cloud of smoke that hung over our heads. 'Your husband is close to recovery Mrs Sherman.' He sat up in his chair. 'Another two weeks is not a long time to wait.'

'Very well... maybe I can bring the children next week.'

'That would be fine,' I said.

'They could visit your friend... seeing as they don't stop talking about her and the damn woods.' She grinned at me.

'No... No Mary the woman is quite unsuitable.'

'Oh mother, don't spoil their fun...' Mary turned her head to me. 'They seem to have fallen for her... charm.' Mary put her tea down on the table. 'Tell me doctor, several of your nurses told me David here relapsed.' She looked across to me. 'Unable, or unwilling to get out of bed, or to wash and shave, in fact became foul mouthed and ill-mannered.'

'Well...' The doctor almost dropped his cup then struggled for the right words. 'David did... and let me say now...' He removed his glasses. 'It was just a couple of days, which is not unusual in the cir...'

'But he *has* recovered...?' Mary did not allow him to finish.

'Yes... yes he has, and not in some small way, down to Mrs Walker.'

'Mrs Walker?' Mary looked at him.

A SEA OF DEAD

'Marlin Walker... The woman you were just talking about.'
Mary looked from the confused doctor to me, I wondered if she noticed the same bemused look on my face.

∽⋙⋘∾

I came across Marlin a day later; she was off to the local farm to get eggs and suchlike, so I asked if I could accompany her.
'If you feel up to it captain, I'm going to the farm then to the post office; have you walked that far lately? I have no wheelchair with me today.'
'You won't need one.' I smiled a reassuring smile.
The day was a fine one, not overly warm but nevertheless pleasant. She wore the grey dress, the one I liked, and she had her hair up which exposed her long smooth neck; somehow I found that arousing.
At the farm, Marlin asked me to wait outside while she went to get her shopping. I turned to face two small children and smiled, yet both just stared at me. I realised why and placed my hand to my jaw; neither child could have been more than nine, both blonde, one a boy, the other a sweet looking girl.
'Who did that?' asked the boy with wide eyes.
'The war...' I replied.
'But who?'

A SEA OF DEAD

'A German.'
'Did you kill him for making you so ugly?'
'No.'
'Why?'
I had no answer.
'Is that your wife?' the boy asked whilst picking his nose.
'No.'
'Won't she marry you because you're ugly?' The girl's voice was full of innocence.
I smiled; I felt unable to continue with this conversation. I heard footsteps behind me.
'Hope they haven't been bothering you sir,' said a woman in her mid-twenties.
'No.' I smiled.
'Come on then,' she said to them both, and they began to walk in the direction of the village, each child straining their neck to keep me in view.
I reached into my coat pocket with trembling fingers, searching for my cigarette packet; yes, I thought to myself, just how ugly must I be? I lit up and sucked in the smoke; how could someone as attractive as Marlin look at me in a romantic way? It would be impossible; I suddenly felt despondent.
'Are you okay?' Marlin asked on her return.
'Fine,' I said putting out my cigarette.
'Let's go then.'
I followed limping; yet another nail in my coffin I thought as I walked alongside her, *'beauty and the beast'*;

A SEA OF DEAD

I made an effort to walk on her left side so as to hide my jaw.

'I need to post a letter.'

'A relative?' I asked.

'Yes my aunt, I need to know if she would be able to put me up.'

'Put you up? But you have a perfectly good cottage to live in.'

'Yes a two bedroom cottage and there is just me, Lady Almina has been good to me, but that cottage needs a family in it, or at least a couple wanting to start one.'

'Surely she will offer you somewhere else on the estate.' I heard the desperation in my voice and wondered if she had.

'All the rooms are needed captain, you should know that, you're in one, and it is only right, I am a single person now, I should not have a cottage to myself.'

'Why?'

'Why? You should know why.'

'I don't understand Marlin, they need you here, I see how good you are with everyone, they all love you, the injured men, the staff... everyone.'

She smiled. 'Yes well that's nice, but I have to make my own way, and maybe it's time to re-start my life again somewhere new.'

I had not noticed we had reached the post office; Marlin went inside where a queue had developed. I stood outside unable to come to terms with what she had just told me.

A SEA OF DEAD

I watched her through the window talking to the other women, I felt *compelled* to watch her; I became transfixed, a thought struck me and I took out my pad and pencil, I then began to sketch her features, unlike the woodland drawing this was not as precise, I needed a study of as many of her facial expressions as possible, I had almost filled an entire page of rough images by the time she came out.

We strolled back slowly; I'm certain she saw that my leg was giving me difficulty and slowed her own pace down to suit mine, the woman was an angel. Marlin spoke about an aunt who lived down by the sea, on what coast she did not say and I foolishly failed to ask, instead I stared enchanted by the different expressions her face made. We parted company outside her cottage; on this occasion I did not mind not being invited inside, I wanted to return to my room to begin work on her portrait.

I shut my door, threw my coat onto the bed and moved the chair to the window, turning it so the light would hit the page at a certain angle. Happy with everything, I sat and began to sketch, turning back to view the rough sketches I had made through the post office window.

I had her sitting with her back to a tree wearing a long white dress open at the neck. I placed her hair up in a bun with countless tiny ringlets falling loosely from it, a garland of flowers around the mass of hair, and another single flower behind one ear. Her facial expression was one of innocence; I had her staring into the distance lost in thought.

Her arms were wrapped around her knees; in her hands she held a posy of wild flowers. I spent another hour just adding the finishing touches; exaggerating her eyes, underlining her cheek bones, placing shadow around her neck, making it the thing of beauty which it was. I wanted to give the impression of a breeze and so allowed the wisps of hair to look as if they were being touched by a light and gentle wind.

It was a labour of love; three or four hours passed and yet it felt like far less. I propped the finished sketch up against the wall and stood back. The more I looked, the more certain I was that it might come to life here in my room, I almost wished for it to happen. I went and lay on the bed before tiredness forced me to fall asleep.

I woke several hours later; a mist had settled over my eyes, on clearing, Marlin's face came into focus. I stared back at the drawing, I felt an urge to get up and go to kiss her face but resisted. I cleared that thought from my mind and sat on the edge of the bed; I took it down and held it in front of me smiling; outside the sun had almost set, then without thinking I stood, picked up my coat and with the pad in my hand left my room.

I was two-thirds of the way to her cottage before I began to think more clearly. It was late; would she want someone turning up at this time? And then I thought of the sketch, she had to see it. Certain she would want to see it, I quickened my step, or as much as my leg would allow me to, and continued to convince myself that I was doing the right thing.

The curtains had been pulled, but I could see that a light was on inside. I made my way down the path towards her front door; inside I felt a hint of anxiety, which I bundled away before it got the better of me. I stood for a moment and took a deep breath, before allowing my knuckles to rap on the door; I waited, listening to the beat of my heart and the sound of my breathing: the world and everything in it stopped.

I began to sense movement coming from within.

'Who is it?' Marlin's voice was full of unease.

'Dav... Captain Sherman.' I spoke softly to reassure her.

'What do you want?' Now there was harshness in her voice.

'I've got something to show you.' It began to dawn on me that this might not be a good idea.

'What?'

'If you open the door I'll...'

'Go away captain,' she interrupted. 'I don't know what possessed you to come out at this time, but I wish you had not.'

My first thought was should I cut my losses and go? But my judgment was that of a madman it seemed.

'I should have waited I know... but now I'm here... please Marlin let me show you then I will go... I do not want to come in I promise.'

A SEA OF DEAD

There was a long silence, the thought crossed my mind she might have gone to bed and left me standing here, except the light remained on.

The next noise I heard was the sliding of a bolt, and then the squeak of the hinges as the door slowly opened. The warm smell of burning wood escaped from the gap in the doorway; she stood wearing a red dress with a white shawl wrapped around her shoulders, the fire created shadows on the walls behind her, if I had had my pencil I would of drawn her again in the firelight.

'What do you want to show me?'
There was no hint of a smile, instead her features were sharp and her eyes narrowed as she looked into my face, I wanted to turn away at that moment, for I now felt her irritation, but I had come too far. I prayed the drawing might soften her as I opened my pad to her page, and turned it so she could see the sketch; I then waited for a reaction which came more swiftly than I thought it might.

'Is this what could not wait?'
Like a fool I just nodded my answer and smiled, she shook her head several times, took a step back and closed the door on me. I did not move, I could almost smell the paint, I felt my warm breath rebound from the wood and heat up my cheeks. Thoughts ran this way and that, like ants on a path going rapidly nowhere, for I was not contemplating her actions... but mine.

Here I was on the doorstep of a woman I hardly knew, who knew even less about me, almost in the middle of the night. Then after forcing her to open her door, I thrust a sketch of her under her nose, before waiting for what? Her to take me in her arms…? Or to tell me how wonderful it was? To decorate my face with kisses in admiration of what I had done? What a fool I had been.

I turned to leave glancing back just once to see if the curtain moved, I was still thinking like a halfwit when the light went out. I wanted to turn the clock back somehow, I remembered coming back into her room and seeing her turning the pages of my pad, I could still remember word for word the compliments she paid me that day. Like the walk in the wood, they had been perfect moments, moments I should treasure; instead I had stained those memories with my sheer act of tactless foolishness.

I had become infatuated by this beautiful woman, but it had also blinded me to the reality of it all. What, if any, encouragement had she shown me? I felt the pain as I admitted to myself *none whatsoever*. And what would attract this handsome woman to me? I felt my jaw at this point and winced with shame.

I had not realised that I had been crying; the realisation of the truth is a hard burden to carry with you. I had forged a path in life without looking where it was leading me and when I *did* look, I found I did not like where it was taking me, except it was too late to turn back; the distance back was longer than the one that stretched out in front of me.

A SEA OF DEAD

Marlin was still young, attractive, intelligent and able to forge her own new route through life. On that walk back I realised that she was never going to allow me to walk that same path, and as much as it hurt me, I had to face up to the truth, but she had made a place in my heart and I knew it would be hard to evict her from it.

※

There was a cool breeze the next morning; I had spotted Marlin going down to where the kitchens were, and decided to wait for her outside however long that took. I wrapped myself up with an extra jumper and positioned myself on a bench which offered the best view of the exit, I then removed my sketch pad to ease away the time.

I foolishly kept looking towards the door every other minute, knowing that she would still be quite some time yet. I found myself sketching blindly, drawing what my mind saw and not my eyes; I felt in a dreamlike state, my mind swum in a lake of silk, as my hand guided the pencil over the paper. I had no idea what my mind had portrayed onto the page, I was blind to the image I had created.

As time went on I began to anticipate her arrival at the doorway; although my pencil continued to draw blindly, its momentum had slowed; and suddenly there she was doing up the buttons of her coat. Marlin looked up towards the sky before setting off; there was no reason to look in my direction which pleased me.

I moved towards her as she set off for home. She walked with the swiftness of someone still young, and I found myself struggling to keep up with her. I was too far away to speak, and did not want to shout my presence behind her, that would have been unthinkable, so I just continued to follow, hypnotized by the swing of her hips.

The pain in my leg increased and I began to fall behind. There was nothing for it, I needed to catch her before she went into her fortress, and I needed the drawbridge down as I had no strength to swim across her moat.

'MARLIN,' I shouted.
She stopped and turned to face me; I prayed for a smile but none appeared; I reached her somewhat out of breath.

'Marlin,' I said again breathing heavily.

'Yes captain...' she replied.

'I'm sorry.'

'Sorry?'

'For last night, I finished the drawing and... well I could not help myself... again I'm so sorry.'

She stared at me; I could see those eyes looking deep into my very soul, there could be no hiding place from that stare, no sanctuary, no place of safety. She searched for a reply to my apology.

'I am sorry.' I felt compelled to break this anxious silence.

'I do not normally forgive this easily captain; in fact I've been known never to speak to those who upset me ever again.'

I shuddered at her words.

'But I will make an exception on this occasion.'

I smiled.

'But tread carefully captain.'

'I will.'

'And by the way... is that how you see me?'

'It is you,' I replied.

'Do you not think you have made me a little too attractive?'

'I'm sorry to say my talent has not the quality to do your beauty justice... the sketch is as close as my meagre ability allows.'

'In your eyes maybe captain, but they seem rose-coloured...'

'No... No... You are that beautiful... I would think to everyone who looks your way.'

She smiled and we stood once more in silence, me looking at her beauty and she at my ugliness.

'I always have a cup of tea when I get in from work, would you like one?'

'Yes please.' My heart leapt for joy.

I sat at the table watching her glide around the kitchen, I studied every movement her body made, the way she tucked a stray piece of hair behind her ear, how she looked with a sense of longing from her window towards the woods, and the smile she gave me when

A SEA OF DEAD

looking across to where I sat; like ice cream left in the sun, my heart melted.

Steam rose upward from the cup she placed in front of me.

'Have you been back into the woods again?' she asked.

'No but I will.' I smiled and looked at her. 'You look tired.'

'Thank you captain, any other observations you wish to make?'

I cursed myself. 'I meant nothing by it...'

'Then why mention it?'

'Why would I not?'

'Because a comment like that infers we are close, which we are not.' She took a sip of her tea. 'What would your wife say?'

Bringing my wife into the conversation was becoming a habit with her, and it was like waving a red rag to a bull, it began to get under my skin.

'I'm speaking to you... not her,' I said with a small amount of bitterness attached.

'Tell me captain... what would your wife say if she knew you were here with me having tea?'

I smiled, I needed to buy some thinking time, but I had a feeling she knew the answer already.

'The girl in the sketch... the French girl...'

I nodded.

'Who was she really?'

'Who I said...'

A SEA OF DEAD

'That's not what I meant... who was she to you?' I smiled and gave her a bewildered look. 'I don't understand.'

'Did you sketch her afterwards?'

I felt my face burn and my mouth became dry.

'Was she another British conquest captain...? Rather young.

I cleared my throat. 'We only stayed for several days; we could hear the bombing coming from the front we were that close to it.'

'Would her father have shot you if you had stayed any longer...? She looks so young captain, is that how you like them... young and innocent, vulnerable, an easy head to turn in your smart uniform? Did you tell her that you were here to save her from the Bosh, to keep her safe?'

I heard the disdain in her voice.

'Sometimes we got scared and lonely.'

'I take it she was not the first?'

I looked away and coughed. 'I'm not proud... I was not thinking straight...'

'Did you sketch her straight afterwards? Your hand seemed steady... how ashamed did you feel? Did you think about your wife and girls when you were... trying not to feel so lonely?'

I remained silent.

'Tell me captain... am I would-be conquest?'

I looked up at her face. *'No!'* I almost shouted. 'No not at all.'

A SEA OF DEAD

She just smiled but said nothing, which had the same effect.

'How can you think that?' I asked.

'I only wondered; it was a simple question... but your reaction makes me think I touched a nerve.' She took another sip of tea and placed the cup gently down on the wooden surface.

'If I have offended you captain, I will apologise.'

'Please call me David.'

'You have my apology; accept one thing at a time... captain.'

I smiled and picked up my cup; from outside a dog barked, inside there was silence.

Marlin suddenly reached across and turned my pad around. 'Let me see it in the daylight.'

She turned the pages over to get to where her portrait was, although she still lingered on the war sketches.

'So this is what you see when you look at me?'

'Yes.'

'It's not what I see when I look in the mirror.'

'No one sees what others do.'

She smiled whilst looking down at the page.

'You are very beautiful,' I whispered.

'You should keep your thoughts to yourself captain.' The smile seemed different, softer.

She flicked back to the young French girl and I felt my body tighten.

'Has your wife ever seen this?'

'No,' I said awkwardly.

A SEA OF DEAD

'Why...? Silly question really.' She smiled and I felt she was teasing me. 'In some way I am flattered that you drew me, but also, part of me wishes you had not.'

'But why?' I said, looking into her eyes again.

'It looks as though I might have been one of your spoils of war, is that the right term?' She flicked back to the sketch of the farmer's daughter. 'Although your taste has become somewhat more mediocre.'

'You are far more attractive than she is.'
She began to laugh. 'Now you think I'm a fool captain.'

'I think nothing of the sort,' I protested. 'I am being truthful.' I slid my fingers slowly through my hair. 'To me you are all I desire... all I want.'

'I see you have forgotten to put in the lines that crisscross my face, missing, I suspect, from her porcelain skin.'

'With age comes a certain quality, an attractive older woman will always turn a head... if there was a crowd of farmer's daughters, you would still stand out in it.' I held her stare.

'Are all men like you?' She smiled.

'You have depth... one minute with you and I was captivated; sensuality is about emotions as well as the physicality. A woman can look young and be sexually attractive, yet while you talk with her, that sexual attraction fades because you find she is shallow; a woman without depth cannot hold your attention for long, no matter how beautiful she may look on the outside, many men look for the woman within.'

A SEA OF DEAD

Marlin began to laugh again, at first it annoyed me but soon it brought a smile to my face.

'And you really believe all that?' she asked in-between wiping the tears of laughter away.

'Yes I do.' I smiled back.

Marlin took the pad and opened it up to the French girl's page and held it up next to her face. 'So you prefer this…' She spoke slowly and deliberately, 'to this?' She pointed her finger at her own face.

'You every time...'

'Then you're either a liar... or blind captain.'

'I am neither.'

'You sketch too well to be blind... so I have to assume you lie to get what you want... Did you tell the girl you loved her to get what you desired...? Maybe not the first time… far too soon...'

'You can fall in love instantly,' I said.

'Really?'

'I did with you.'

Outside the sun cast a shadow across the land as it slipped behind a cloud, the room darkened for a moment then as it reappeared, the room brightened; inside our silence seemed almost deafening.

She rose from her chair and took both cups back to the sink where she stood for a moment looking out of the window.

'You should go captain.'

'I'm sorry.'

'Then why did you say it?'

A SEA OF DEAD

'Because I felt I wanted to tell you... to let you know.'

'Did you not once consider what I would think? Or is this all about you?'

'Again I'm sorry,' I repeated.

'And so am I... I am not young and naive, nor am I French...'

'They were not my intentions.'

'Here... take your sketch pad and go captain...'

She picked it up to hand to me, except it fell open on the table to the last page, the one I was working on while I waited for her earlier.

'Is this what you really think of me?'

I looked down at the open page, unable at first, to recognise my own work, but it was Marlin's face that stared out of the page, as beautiful as I had ever seen her, except below that face she was naked.

'I didn't realise I had...'

'Captain, go.'

'Marlin, *please* believe me... I must have...'

Marlin was looking away from me; what had been a perfect day was becoming yet another nightmare. If Marlin was shocked then so was I, for I knew it was my hand that had guided the pencil across the page, but I had done it blindly, her first look at it had been mine as well, except how could I make her see that.

'Marlin...'

'Go.'

A SEA OF DEAD

'I wish I had not done that... but it does capture you and all your beauty.'

'I look like a common whore.'

'No... No you don't.'

'Anyone picking up this pad, will think that I posed for that drawing... will they not?'

'I suppose.'

'And what would they think of me? A woman who has known a man for five minutes and takes her clothes off to allow him to draw her.'

'Put like that... it does look bad but...'

'Give me that page before you go captain.'
I stared down at it, I could not refuse, but it seemed a pity for I had never drawn as well and would never do so again.

'Captain...' She held out her hand.

I tugged at the page but it would not move; what I was doing felt so wrong, the drawing was one of beauty and I had no intention of showing it to anyone. I had not set out to upset Marlin, but it seemed that every time we came together I appeared to do so; I felt so despondent. A round wet splash landed on the page, followed by another then another, my tears flowed and I had no way of stopping them, I had witnessed so much ugliness that I could not destroy something of such beauty.

I went to tear the page again, but suddenly found a hand covering my own; I looked up into her face and attempted to smile, but an overwhelming sense of pure emotion overtook me, and I broke down and cried. She pulled me into her body and I laid my head on her shoulder; as she held me I felt fear and despair flood from my body.

I sensed the beating of her heart and suddenly realised how lonely I had been, and how safe her arms were making me feel. We remained like this for several minutes before she moved her head away.

'Are you alright?' Her voice was a whisper.

'Yes... sorry.'

'Don't be,' she whispered.

'But I am, for the drawing, for how I am, for being such a fool these past weeks... you must hate me.'

'I'm trying to unravel you captain,' she said still holding me. 'You're a mass of knots, when I undo one, there's another, then another... Hate is too strong a word... but you are certainly annoying at times... and yet at times...' She stopped and wiped a tear from her own cheek.

I surprised myself by pulling away first, I could have remained like this for hours; I too wiped away the moisture from my cheeks and tried to focus on her face.

'I have seen many men come apart at the seams, and I can understand why many fall for the nurses who comfort them... but it...' she whispered.

'I am in love with you... I know I am.'

She took a step back. 'But you do not know me.'

'I do.'

A SEA OF DEAD

She almost broke into a laugh. 'How? By drawing me... did you see into my soul captain...? And what did you see?'

'I saw a wonderfully brave woman who bares the scar of a lost love... and who is continuing with her life, not wanting anyone to feel sorry for her, never looking for pity or hiding away behind a look of despondency, and it makes people like me have so much admiration for someone like you.'

'Enough.' She placed a hand over my mouth. 'You are a married man and should not be talking like this to me... please stop.'

'And you do not feel anything for me?' I moved towards her.

She took a step back. 'No; stay away.'

'But...'

'No... I think you should go now.' She looked like she was about to break down in tears.

'I can't.'

'Don't you see you are distressing me...? Now please go; if you have those feelings for me then you will leave me now, I thought love was about being unselfish captain.'

I moved to the door and turned around, but said nothing to her, I had nothing *to* say, and then I left. Halfway up the path I remembered my pad, but I was not going to go back for it now, it would have to wait for another day.

A SEA OF DEAD

∼⚬∽

I did not see Marlin the next day, I wanted some time to lapse before doing so and I needed that time to think. Mary and her mother were down with the children tomorrow, I wondered if she was going to ask Marlin to have the girls again; the thought did not fill me with as much fear as it done had before.

My session with Doctor Longhorn went well; in fact it went too well. 'We could bring your release date forward Captain Sherman.' He had smiled; I put on a serious face and stated that I felt *'I needed a bit more time'* and *'that the nightmares were still interrupting my sleep.'* In fact, just that night I had slept badly; Marlin's face had been replaced by faded images of the war.

I was aware of crawling through thick slimy mud, with the stench of death all around me. I passed lifeless eyes, open stomachs with their guts hanging out, I wiped my face only to look at my blood covered hand; I passed a head without a body, a face without its eyes, a leg without a foot, and when I looked up, I saw this sea of atrocity stretch to the horizon.

I awoke the coward I had gone to sleep; I saw Private Young looking at me, he knew, his eyes told me, I drew them once on the back of a fag packet, I gave him large open eyes, like I witnessed on dead men, simply because all of us were halfway to becoming dead men

A SEA OF DEAD

ourselves, but I had rubbed them out so he could no longer see me when I went to sleep.

I drew all of them, all the dead men making them all immortal. They would remain alive, albeit on a piece of paper, but they would live. I had promised to send them to their families back home, to my shame I never kept that promise, instead I kept them to look at, to remind myself that I was the only one who survived, but by keeping those images it meant they too survived with me.

That feeling of sickness which always appeared before my mother-in-law arrived was already simmering inside me. I drew on my cigarette and blew a cloud of smoke out. I heard a scream, then a girl's yell; I turned and saw Trudy and Lizzy making their way towards me, followed closely by Marlin, and further back, Mary and her mother. I waited for both girls to reach me.

'We're going to the woods papa,' Lizzy squealed. Trudy smiled and held on to Marlin's hand. 'Marlin is going to put my hair up like hers.'

'That's nice,' I whispered looking at Marlin. Mary finally arrived. 'Are you ready David?' she asked. 'We have booked a lovely place in town.'

'Plenty of time,' I said.

I looked at Marlin again, I wondered if she felt awkward with Mary so close, particularly after the things I had said when we were last together. Did she wish I was staying so I could go to the woods with them too? I doubted she did.

A SEA OF DEAD

'Will you be okay?' Mary said to Marlin.
'Fine,' she replied.
'Very well let us go.'
We parted there; Marlin and the girls proceeded across the grass towards the cottages and woods; I watched them go and how I envied them, I felt contempt for Mary as strongly as I felt love for Marlin, how could life be so cruel?

≼ঌ

All through dinner I thought about Marlin. We sat in a well-lit dining room surrounded by another eight or so tables, all, it seemed, full of smiling faces. The sound of voices and the scraping of china dominated the area around us. But it seemed that every time I looked up, someone was looking back at me, or was it my imagination? A woman on the nearest table pulled a strange face when her eyes came into contact with my face, while a young girl of no more than twelve kept touching her own jaw with her fork.

I had to have a glass of wine; although Mary did not want me to, I argued far too loudly, so making her give in to me; Mary hated scenes. I then forced her into another, I had not drunk alcohol in six months and it seemed to go straight to my head. I poked my tongue out at the girl. To everyone else who stared at me, I decided I would stare straight back at them.

A SEA OF DEAD

Now they no longer just looked, but, behind hands, whispered to each other. A man in a brown suit did not bother to hide the fact, instead he told another gentleman on his table that people that looked like me, should not be allowed in restaurants.

'I wish you would wear your uniform David,' whispered Mary; she had noticed but chose, as always, to say nothing.

'Why?' I asked taking another large mouthful of the red house wine.

'You look nice in it.'

'And will that make it more acceptable for all these people in here who want to stare at me?' My voice grew louder.

'Shhh David,'

'No... But I would like an answer... Would my face be acceptable if I wore a uniform?'
Whispers sprang up from every table.

'David *please*...'
Mary's mother had her trusty handkerchief out and was dabbing her nose looking flustered.

'Well let me tell you why I am not wearing my uniform darling.' My voice grew loud above the noise in the room once again. 'It's because it has not been cleaned, it still has thick mud, some shit, blood and brain stains all over it.'
The sound of cutlery hitting china along with gasps of breath could be heard around the room. I smiled while I surveyed the room.

A SEA OF DEAD

'How lucky they are... the dead, because we living have to return to be gawped at like some freak circus act.' I stood and raised my glass. 'Let's have a toast for all those brave men who have had their brains blown out for the likes of you lot.'

'David for *God's* sake...' Mary tugged at my jacket.

'Mary, I feel a turn coming on,' said her mother draining of colour.

'Sir,' said the man in the brown suit, 'some respect please, there are women and children in here.'

'Do they not want to drink to our fine men sir?'

'If you *are* a British soldier sir, then you are a disgrace to Her Majesty's uniform, if I were younger sir... I would flog you.'
I smiled at him. 'If I had a gun... *sir*... I would shoot you *dead*... you pompous old bastard.'
A waiter moved towards our table sweating profusely, as the volume of noise increased.

'Would sir please sit?'
I looked across at the old bastard in the brown suit. His face a furious red, he had remained standing.

'I'll sit when he does.' I said pointing in his direction. 'You people have no idea... we slept in piss and shit, we woke to find rats the size of cats chewing at our coats and boots, then soaked, sick and exhausted, they sent us over the top to be massacred, simply because it was our turn. The next day the Bosh would do the same, then ours again and so on. Each side blowing the other's fucking brains out.' There was no stopping me now, I looked down at Mary who looked away, her mother was curled into a ball, the wine had flooded my senses, what needed saying I was about to say.

'As you run across no man's land, over the sharp barbed wire fencing, through blood filled bomb holes, you see the man in front of you lose his head, another an arm, but you still keep going simply because one of your own officers will shoot you if you do not. Now there you have it, the Germans one side wanting to shoot you, and your own officers behind wanting to do the same.' I drained another glass staring at the man in the brown suit, and held it up high, like some cup I had won at cricket.

'You crawl over the man you played cards with last night, who will never deal another hand simply because he has no arms now, you blow your whistle urging your men in the slaughter that is happening all around you... you urge them on to their death, and when you return you feel fortunate... except suddenly you feel cheated.' I swallowed the last of the wine in my glass to a hushed room.

A man I took to be the manager, dressed in a nice clean black suit bent his head down to Mary's ear, and whispered something.

'We have to go,' she said standing, 'come on Mother.'

'Who is he?' I asked.

'The manager.'

A SEA OF DEAD

I looked at the man who was a short fellow, no older than fifty; his hair was thinning on top and grey around the edges. His forehead was covered in sweat and I could see he was breathing heavily.

'Is a captain from the British Army not welcome in your establishment after fighting for King and Country?'

'Sir I would like you to leave please.'

'And the reason?'

'David... *please...*' Mary stood with her arm outstretched towards me.

'You are upsetting the customers sir...'

'No, I think you have it all wrong... your so called *customers* are upsetting me'

Mary put her face into her hands, while her mother began to cry.

I flung my napkin down and went to walk away only for my bad leg to get caught up in the tablecloth; I found myself heading face first towards the floor, I reached out and grasped anything to break the fall, which pulled the entire contents of our table down on top of me.

I lay there for a minute or so unable or unwilling to move; in my mind I saw Marlin sitting at the table with a massive smile fixed to her face, then she began to laugh and I began to laugh with her. I stood up and brushed myself down meeting the eyes of those around the room.

'Good afternoon.' I smiled. 'Please continue.'

I followed Mary and her mother outside to the sound of voices: *'Drunken fool.'* *'Damn disgrace.'* Then I stood

A SEA OF DEAD

outside and breathed in the fresh air; Mary and her mother both stood staring at me.

I took out a cigarette. 'I was defending my unit,' I said as I struck my match.

Both tuned their backs on me.

✧✧

  The cottage looked empty as we arrived back; I assumed it would be, as we had only been gone for half the time we expected. We had made the twenty minute trip in near silence, except for Mary's mother tutting every half mile. As for me, I was glad to be going back, I had had quite enough of feeling like a fish in a bowl, I longed for the peace and tranquillity of the estate, but mainly the comfort of the woods and Marlin.

  Mary told the driver to wait while we went to fetch the children.

  'Mother, stay here.'

  'No... No... I can't leave you,' she said looking at me.

I began to walk to the window and Mary went straight up to the front door and knocked on it.

  'Where are they?' she muttered to herself.

  'In the wood I would have thought,' I said trying to work out why there was a suitcase on the wooden kitchen table; I felt troubled by its presence.

A SEA OF DEAD

Mary told her mother to wait, but again she took no notice and followed at a snail's pace. We had only walked for a minute when we heard the girl's screams.

'Mary... Mary... that's the girls,' screamed Mary's mother. 'What's wrong?'

'That, mother-in-law, is the sound of children enjoying themselves.' I smiled at her.

I saw Trudy first, all smiles and covered in dirt, holding a bunch of wild flowers. I would love to have sketched her right at that moment, I had never seen her so happy, so childlike still, I wanted to capture it somehow and I wondered what she would be like in a year.

'Daddy these are for you.'

'Trudy, look at your coat.' Mary's voice carried through the afternoon.

Trudy looked down at the stains then back up at her mother, she smiled and I laughed out loud. Lizzy was now coming, holding Marlin's hand, in the other she held something small which she would not take her eyes from. Marlin smiled down at her; how beautiful they looked together.

Mary's mother finally arrived. 'Do you see what you have done to my grandchildren's clothes young lady?' She stared at Marlin.

'It will wash out,' replied Marlin. 'I asked Mrs Sherman if I could take them back into the woods.' She looked at Mary waiting for a response, none came. 'You said that would be fine.' Again she waited for Mary to agree or not.

'But that does not mean you should deliberately get them dirty,' said Mary's mother.

'Children don't stay clean in woods.' Marlin smiled. 'Not while they are enjoying themselves.'

'It does not matter mother,' said Mary looking flustered.

'Does not matter... What have you there Elizabeth?'

Lizzy ran forward and opened her hand, on it sat a caterpillar.

'Mary quick before it bites her; remove it...'

'It won't bite Gran,' said Lizzy smiling. 'I'm calling it Fred.'

'You throw it away child, *now*... Mary, please let us go and bring the children before they catch something; I will run a bath the moment we get back. The very moment... please hurry Mary.'

'You're back early,' said Marlin, wiping the back of Trudy's coat.

'A small disagreement,' I replied.

Lizzy released the caterpillar after Marlin had whispered something in her ear. I felt uneasy about my children's future, fun had been taken out of it, and they will continue to be deprived of it, Marlin had done more in a short time than anyone could have wished for, yet I doubted they would be seeing her again.

Both girls had discovered a new world, an exciting world, they would have years to sit around dressed up at dinner parties, at weddings, but now was the time to be children, to laugh, to make a noise, to have fun, this time will pass so quickly; soon they will see the world for what it is, wars and greed.

Lizzy pulled away from Mary's mother who was attacking her with her white handkerchief saying *'cleanliness is next to godliness.'* Both children ended up wrapped around Marlin's legs.

'Is daddy not coming?' they asked.

'No... No not today... say goodbye.'

The real world when it crept into her neat and orderly life unsettled her, being shielded from the worst life could offer was her downfall. Its reality came as a shock, now she would return to the safety of her father's money and high walled estate; I shuddered to think both my children could end up the same.

Mary walked up to me while her mother shepherded the children into the automobile.

'I think we should talk David.'

'I have no problem with that.'

'And with Doctor Longhorn in attendance...'

'Why?'

'So he can assess you... David you are not yourself, you need medical help, you also owe mother an apology, and God knows what father will say, but first you, I think you might need special help David... help they can't give you here, I will talk to father.'

'Hold on... I'm not mad Mary... far from it, I've had my eyes opened and...'

A SEA OF DEAD

'Not now David...' With that she turned and walked to the car saying nothing to Marlin.
The children waved goodbye as the car moved off, Marlin and I waved back, I felt good standing next to her.

'It seems you're my last friend.' I spoke without looking in Marlin's direction.

'I'm the only one here captain.'

'I was talking to you,' I said with a smile.

'Really...'

She turned and walked away.

'Where are you going?' I asked.

'For a walk...'

I followed without asking where.

⊷⊶

Marlin found the worn path instantly and began to follow it, I remained several steps behind.

'Are you going somewhere?' I asked.

She did not answer but continued on her way, before stopping next to a large oak tree at the point where the path bent.

'Yes,' she said without looking at me.

'When...? Where...?'

'I am not your wife captain... should you have not asked her that? She seemed to leave in a hurry.'

'I don't care where she is going... but I do you.'

'Don't.'

A SEA OF DEAD

'I can't help it.' I wanted to grab her arm and turn her to face me, I wanted to kiss her mouth and see what would happen, but I was still very much a coward.

'You seem to have a habit upsetting females captain, is it something you practise?' I saw the smile form on her lips. 'And your father-in-law it seems is going to be very angry with you.'

'Damn him,' I said.

'You're full of aggression captain.'

I picked up a stick and snapped it in half. 'You still have not told me where you're going Marlin.'

'And I'm not about to.'

'Why?'

'Why do you want to know?'

The breeze brought the smell of lavender in my direction; I breathed it in before answering.

'So I can come.'

She laughed out loud. 'How presumptuous of you captain, or did you assume I wanted you to escort me? Have I led you to believe that is what I wanted?'

'No.' I felt my heart sink and my mouth go dry. 'Why now?' I asked.

'Why *not* now?'

'Do you always answer a question with a question?'

'Do you always ask so many?'

I smiled as she placed some loose hair behind her ear.

'Sometimes.'

'Sometimes what?'

A SEA OF DEAD

'I ask too many questions.'
She grinned as she bent down to pick up what looked like a small stone.

'Tell me captain, do you believe in spirits?'

'Those that are drunk or...'

'You have a sense of humour then... I was wondering... Well?'

'I have an open mind.'

'Hedging your bets captain, waiting for me to tell you what I think, afraid to speak your own mind.'

'No, but what has this to do with you leaving?'

She walked in a circle around the tree trailing her hand across the bark.

'My Alan is everywhere here, these woods, the cottage, even in the main house; I can almost feel him touch me.'

'In that case,' I interrupted, 'why would you want to leave here?'
She leant her back against the tree, she looked so perfect.

'I love how it makes me feel, and like you say why would I want to lose that feeling?'
Again the breeze rose, and I felt it kiss both our faces.

'One day I was walking to the village and felt him next to me, he was right there just like the day you walked with me.' She walked a couple of steps away. 'He sat beside me as you sketched the other day.'
I shuddered at that thought.

A SEA OF DEAD

'Then I realised he is everywhere with me, it's not just this wood, or the cottage, it is wherever *I* am, so if I want to begin again he will go wherever I go.'

'So do I take it you will always remain in mourning?'

'No captain, there you go again, it's not all about you.'

'I didn't mean it like that.'

'*How* then?'

'If Alan is there with you every day and... every night, how can you forge a new relationship?'
She laughed out loud. 'With you?'

'I did not say that.'

'But you thought it.'

'If it was with me then... how would it...'

'It would make no difference, there is a large place in my heart for Alan, but there is room for another if I so choose. I know Alan would want me to be happy, because he was not a selfish man captain, he always thought of me first. The person who wants me will have to except Alan, it's that simple.'

I could see she had thought this through, her clarity of thinking astounded me, she was so certain of everything, she left no stone unturned and that made the panic spread through me at a fast rate of knots. After my children, she was what I desired most in the world, to lose her now would be like abandoning half of my life.

'Come away with me Marlin.' I almost shouted.

'With you?'

A SEA OF DEAD

'Yes.'

'No...' She looked directly at me. 'I need a man I can trust.'

'I am that man.'

'Captain, how many indiscretions did you commit while you were in France serving King and Country?'
I could not hold her stare. 'We were in the middle of a war.'

'So war made cheating on your wife acceptable?'
I walked away and looked across the meadow to where the wood began again. 'War is a lonely business... sometimes we seek comfort.'

'And your wife, she gets lonely too and what if she seeks the same... comforts?'

'That is different her life is not at risk, she is not living with the fear that her life could be taken at any moment.'

Marlin breathed in deeply, looked up to the sky and smiled before looking back at me.

'Why do men make the rules to suit themselves or change them to suit the game?'

'War is no game.'

'No, before Alan deteriorated, he talked about the generals who played war games using the men as pawns like they were on a giant chessboard.'
I smiled, I could not argue with him; those idiots who remained dry and well fed five miles behind the lines, moved bits of paper around a table that represented the fathers, sons and husbands who made up their army,

having no idea about what they were doing, or the consequences of their decisions and the lives that would be sacrificed; the children made fatherless, the widows left to struggle on and the mothers who wept, trying to understand why.

To these people death was an unfortunate consequence of war; casualties and war went together like a horse and cart. They would sit down again with the brandy bottle open and come up with yet another harebrained scheme for their obedient army to implement.

'Don't you think I don't know that...? These orders were given to people like me, for me to make men like Alan carry them out at the sound of my whistle, and to go marching to their deaths.' I kicked at a stone on the ground. 'Shopkeepers, farmers, road sweepers, factory workers who knew nothing of war, but just carried out orders without question... and most of those orders were bad, which meant most did not return, and then people like me wrote letters to people like you to tell them how brave their husband, son, father had been... so *yes*, I wickedly sort comfort with a bottle of scotch and a woman.'

I leaned with one hand on the trunk of a tree; overhead a bird sung, in the far distance a bell tolled, after all, this was England at peace, the war was somewhere else, if you could not see or hear it then it did not exist, like those in the restaurant today, war had its place, but a restaurant is not one of them, neither should a

A SEA OF DEAD

man's injuries be displayed, it was a lowering of standards and we are British.

'Did all men act as you did?' Marlin stood next to me.

'Not all.'

'No?'

'Those of us who knew what was happening or what was about to happen.'

'So not all?'

'Not your Alan, if that's what you're thinking.'

'Why not? What makes you so certain?'

'Because of you.'

'Me?'

'You say you feel his spirit.' I turned to face her. 'Even now... then he would have felt you with him at all times... I am certain of it.'

'Then why was my spirit not enough to save him?'

'Because it was his time.'

'How final captain... always the solider.'

'Do not call me that.'

'Are you still not one deep inside?'

'No, let me come with you and you can see for yourself.'

'Why should I allow someone who helped take away my only love...? Why should I let you come away with me and be a constant reminder?' I stood. 'I did not say that it was me.'

'No... But someone *like* you.'

'But not me.'

'How many wives and mothers are out there who could blame you captain?'

I had no answer for I had asked myself the same question a thousand times.

'Anyway,' she went on, 'you have a life here.'
I shook my head. 'I have an existence,' I whispered.

'A wife and two beautiful girls,' said Marlin.

'I have nothing.'

'Are you about to wallow in self-pity again captain?'

'Let me draw you?' I asked.

'You have done so already.' She stared at me.

'Please.'
She seemed to contemplate my pleading instead of rejecting it out of hand.
'Tomorrow captain.'

'Does that mean you are not leaving yet?' I felt a small ray of hope.

'No captain, not yet.'

'When then?'
She smiled.

⁂

We arranged to meet at the cottage after she finished work, we decided on 3 o'clock, which meant I had tomorrow to convince her to let me accompany her to wherever she was bound. How I was to achieve that God only knew. But if the pounding in my heart and the ache in my head was anything to go by, to live without her would be almost impossible.

I had an unusual note left for me by Doctor Longhorn when I returned to my room, inviting me to a meeting in his office the day after tomorrow at 10.30am. Nothing had been scheduled until the following Wednesday, by then my intention was to be elsewhere with Marlin. But first I had another mission to perform; I took my jacket from behind the door and made my way down to reception. I needed to be shown the records for this great house which had been put into storage.

≈≈

I slept well and ate a hearty breakfast before taking coffee on the terrace. Marlin had already begun work and an image of her flashed up in my mind. How lucky her husband had been. To be loved by her, must have seemed to him like some extravagant dream; to be loved by any woman is an amazing feeling, but to be loved by Marlin was surely the supreme miracle.

For some reason I thought of Private Young asking me to sketch him perched above the trench.

'Don't be silly man…' I told him, 'some damn sniper will blow your brains out.'
He looked at me and smiled. 'I know,' he replied.

A SEA OF DEAD

I did sketch him, along with most of the others in the squad; they wanted me to send the sketches home if anything happened to them. One by one they all got killed, yet I did not send even one of the sketches for I felt in some way responsible for their deaths; it was I who passed on the orders, and it was my whistle that had dispatched them to their deaths.

I walked to the cottage at a leisurely pace, arriving just after three. I was only halfway down the path when her door opened; I watched as she stepped out into the sunlit afternoon. She had let her hair down, I had never seen her like this and although she still possessed that charm, I felt it acted as a cloak hiding her natural beauty.

'Would you put your hair up when I come to draw you?' I asked.

'Yes captain, I have pins in my pocket.'
I thought she was going to say more; instead her lips remained firmly together. We continued in silence, each of us it seemed, consumed with our own thoughts. The afternoon sky was a patchwork of blue and white; a breeze stirred the top of the trees, but only a gentle waft made its way to ground level.

We came to an old wooden gate, I went up and gave it a pull, making certain of its stability. I asked if I could draw her seated on it, behind was the perfect backdrop. The branches of a tree on one side hung down forming an arch, while a bush grew wild the other. A tall oak stood in the middle of the field behind, and so I set my angle to integrate it into the sketch, leaving a space to one side.

When I was happy I breathed in deeply, the sound of birds singing, and the creaking of branches high above us, formed an ambience where just the two of us existed. War was unthinkable in these surroundings, the world as a whole could not penetrate this setting. A rabbit looked at us from the field behind, making me smile back at him, before taking my place under another tree.

'Are you comfortable?' I asked.

'Yes very.'

Marlin sat on my coat for comfort, her long dress with its creases spilled across her lap. She had, as promised, pinned her hair up, allowing some of it to fall loose at my request. She placed her hands together in her lap; from below the dusty pink material of her dress, black lace edging sat above black ankle boots which were tightly laced up to the lower part of her shins.

'Then I will begin,' I said.

Marlin nodded her head, at that very moment, the sun edged from behind a cloud bathing us in golden sunshine.

I worked like I had never done before; my concentration was such that I had not noticed a squirrel sitting behind me watching my pencil gliding across the paper. I worked with feverish urgency, I wanted to capture every feature, for my pencil to outline her beauty which was obvious to the naked eye, but how was I to illustrate that which was concealed within? The flawless beauty of her character; the captivating charm which drew you in, wrapping itself around you, suffocating you with her beguiling presence into submission. I had to do my best to convey how I felt about her.

When I was almost done, I pulled from my pocket what I had discovered last night. I held it at the top of the page with my thumb, my eyes made sporadic glances up to it. This had to be perfect; I could not accept anything mediocre. I sat back and stretched my arms and felt the tightness that inflicted pain down one side.

'May I see?' she asked.

I had sat on a small tree stump; when I rose the pain increased tenfold, forcing me to wince.

'Are you alright captain?'

'Yes. Yes, I'm fine.' I smiled through gritted teeth. 'Let me sign it first.'

As I did so, Marlin got down from the fence, straightening out the fabric of her dress. She also stretched her back, moving her neck from side to side in an effort to free it from stiffness. I put the name *Sherman* in the bottom corner, before quickly shading in some shadow I had missed. Finally I handed it to her and stood back with my heart pounding.

There was no initial reaction, instead her stare seemed to intensify, but it remained for the time being without emotion. For several seconds panic filled my thoughts, sweat formed around my collar and I reached for my cigarettes, lighting one instantly. I took a large mouthful of smoke into my lungs and waited. Then she looked up at me and a single tear left each eye, they rolled slowly down towards her cheeks, hovering for a moment before picking up speed, coming to rest together and embracing on her chin.

'I...' I felt the need to speak.
She held her hand up in order to stop me.
'When...? How...?'
'I went to reception last night, and asked if they had any staff photographs going back five or six years. They were very helpful; I asked them to point Alan out which they did, whereupon I made this small sketch of him. When your sketch was complete I just added him leaning on the gate next to you.'

I held my breath, I had nothing more to say, either she was going to like it or she was going to hate me.

'I'm sorry if I...' Once again I tried to speak.
'No... No... It's perfect... Thank you captain, thank you very much.' She looked up; several more tears had joined those original ones.
If beauty could be measured in time, then a thousand years passed me by as she stood there in all her overpowering allure.

'Here.' She handed me the pad while she searched for a handkerchief tucked up into her sleeve.

I looked again at my work, studied their faces and wondered if I had captured their happiness, I prayed I had. From Marlin's reaction I probably had. We began our walk back in silence; Marlin's eyes continued to spill over with tears, flowing like rain on a window pane down her face, I looked away guilty that I was the cause of it.

'Marlin...'

'Yes?' She looked sideways at me.

'I won't get in your way...' I swallowed hard. 'I can find a place close to you, I will apply no pressure, maybe... maybe after a time, a year if that's how long it takes, we can see how things are, if you have any feelings for...'

'Captain,' she whispered, 'I do like you, as much as you annoy and upset me at times, but we are not compatible, we are so different...'

'We are not so very different.' I started to plead with her.

'We are, we are very different, either I will drive you away or you...'

'No, no you could never drive me away Marlin, I love you too much.'

'Now you do... or you think you do, but what in six months time, a year, what then? And what about your children captain have you not thought about them in all this?'

'I've thought of nothing else, do you think I am doing this lightly...? They will come and visit.'

'Visit…' She suddenly stopped walking. 'Will that be enough?'

'Yes... that and having you to look at every day.'

She stood staring at me before looking up towards the sky, she closed her eyes and I took my chance, I felt I had nothing to lose, my lips touched hers and I held her loosely around the waist, either she was going to pull away, or her arms would fold around me. In the middle of this illusion I remembered my ugliness, and it was me who pulled away first, touching my hand to my wound.

'Sorry... I don't know what... sorry...'
She stood looking at me. 'Was I doing something wrong captain?'

'No, no you did nothing wrong,' I whispered.

'Then why did you stop? Were you thinking about your wife?'

'NO!'

'Are you sure?'

'Why did you allow me to do that?' I asked still with my hand on my jaw.

'I don't know, I wish I could answer you captain, maybe it has been a long time since I've been held, maybe you reminded me of what it is like to feel wanted.'

'I see.'

'Now answer me,' she said. 'Why do you cover your jaw like that?'

'I feel so... ugly.'
She smiled. 'Do you think me shallow captain?'

'No.'

'If you had seen Alan during those last months you would have wondered how I could have touched him. His face was almost unrecognisable as the man who had left to go to war. Like some of these here captain, with parts of their features blown away, because if you have any compassion for people, or love as I did in Alan's case, or if you are fond of...'

'As in my case,' I interrupted.
She stopped and smiled again. 'Possibly captain, possibly.'
I smiled back.

'We should look beyond the physical when we love, people's qualities are more important; their decency, principles, the goodness in their heart, they are the qualities I look for captain, not, as you think, the physical.'

'What are you saying to me?' I asked.

'I still do not know whether I could trust you.'

'Trust me?'

'The farmer's daughter, but of course that was war.'

'I would never do that to you.'

Marlin stepped away, I could see she was deep in thought and did not want to interrupt her.

'I will go alone captain...'

'But...'

She held up her hand to stop my outburst. 'I will go alone, I will not be the one who they point the finger at, if your marriage is over then you end it the right way, think about your children. As for us, I would not mind seeing you again captain, visit me, talk to me, let's see if we can grow, but remember you will never be to me what Alan was, and if you cannot accept that, then stay away from me, because you will only risk hurting yourself, but captain, I give you no promises.'

A SEA OF DEAD

I breathed out a sigh, unable to take in all that she had said. So instead of being rejected, she was giving me an opportunity to redeem myself; to do this the right way, a chance to get to know her, maybe to love her as I wanted to? I would make certain that I would follow the rules of her game to the letter, I could not lose what I never thought could ever be mine.

'Yes, I will do whatever you say Marlin, if there is a chance to spend the rest of my life with you, then I need not be in such a rush. I will make certain that my marriage is ended harmoniously, my children and I see as much of each other as is humanly possible afterwards, and that you are in no way implicated.'

She began to walk on in silence, I followed one step behind, and the consequence of what we had discussed only now fully hit me. For a moment the future terrified me, I became panicky and felt my face flush; from the first time I saw her, all I had wanted was to be with her all the time and now here I was apprehensive about the possibility.

'When are you going? I asked, now by her side.

'Tomorrow morning.'

'Tomorrow…?' I grabbed her arm and turned her towards me. *'Tomorrow?'* I said again looking into her beautiful face.

'Yes captain... tomorrow.'

'But we have so much to talk about, can't you delay it.'

'No it's not possible.'

'Why?'

'Because, the cottage will be the home of a new couple the day after tomorrow.'

'So where are you to go Marlin? Please tell me.' She looked into my eyes and I immediately felt nervous.

'Go home captain and sleep on what I have said.'

'But...'

'Captain... Listen to me please... sleep on what we have spoken about, I do not leave for the station until 10.30 in the morning, come before, tell me you are still of the same mind, then I will give you the address of where you can find me.'

'Marlin, why not just tell me now? I'm not going to change how I feel.' I almost laughed. 'I am yours from now on.'

'I don't want to *own* you captain, I want an equal partner in life, but I will not change my mind; tomorrow… and we will continue as planned. Remember captain I still think of the French girl, and although this is not war, I need convincing that you are what you say you are.'

'I am.'

'Tomorrow captain.' She spoke as we reached the cottages.

We did not kiss before we parted, I foolishly leaned my head towards her, but on this occasion she moved hers away.

'I was foolish once captain, it will not happen again, I will make you earn the right next time.'

A SEA OF DEAD

I smiled and bowed my head.

'Until tomorrow,' I said about to turn away.

'Here...' I held my sketch pad out towards her.'

'Are you certain?'

'Why not, I will get it back soon.'

She smiled at me. 'One thing before you go...'

'Yes?'

She opened the pad to her drawing. 'I need you to sign it.'

'I have.' Her finger then pointed to the bottom of the page.

'Could you sign it...? David...'

I did as she asked.

⋙⋘

My ashtray overflowed with butts after a sleepless night. I had sat on the edge of my bed, or stood looking out on darkness, where I could just make out the hilltops against a lightening sky, seeing tree tops sway gently in a light breeze. Inside I felt on edge, as if I had forgotten to do something important, but could not think what it was. My head felt dizzy and my chest tight, I even questioned what I was doing, which made me feel nauseous, *'nerves'* I said to myself aloud.

I was certain the constant pounding of my heart could not be normal, maybe I should mention it to Doctor Longhorn in the morning, or perhaps I should not, I was sure I could do a pretty good job of diagnosing the problem myself. I lay on top of the bed thinking, and then woke to find morning had crept up on me when I was not looking.

I lit up another cigarette and buried my face in my hands, I had never felt so tired in all my life, and considering my time in the trenches I found that hard to believe. I looked at my watch, 8.50, I had time to wash and freshen up before my meeting with Longhorn, prior to setting off to the cottage.

I filled the basin wondering how I had ever questioned what I was doing, I had never been so certain of anything before. I submerged my face in clear cold water and allowed it to remain there for a good minute, I gasped in air as I rose, and the sensation woke me from my fatigued state. Feeling fresh I began to dress, I think I even whistled a tune, today felt like the beginning of a new chapter in my life, I had up until then forgotten about my jaw, that was until I looked in the mirror to shave.

I managed to throw that feeling of despondency off, I had to look forward and not behind me, the past was the past and now I had a second chance to be happy. Shaved, washed and dressed I made my way down to Longhorn's office on the ground floor. I was on time which for me was unusual and I was smiling to myself when greeting his secretary.

'Good morning captain,' she said smiling back, probably thinking my smile had been for her. 'They are waiting inside.'

'They?' I repeated.

'Yes...' Then she suddenly stopped speaking. I did not press her; instead I rapped my knuckles on the door and entered.

Longhorn rose as usual from behind his desk, placing a cigarette into his ashtray. Uncharacteristically, he did not walk around the desk to greet me, but instead stood straightening his jacket and clearing his throat.

'David,' he said with unease.

It was at that point I noticed we were not alone, two men stood by the window gazing out onto the grounds, on the other side of the room Mary sat with another man who I recognised but could not put a name to. I heard a movement from behind and turned to see another two men.

'Have I forgotten something doctor?' I said. 'Is it your birthday? If so I have forgotten to bring you anything.'

'No... No David, let me introduce these people.' He sat muttering something about all this being most irregular. 'You of course know your wife,' he went on. I felt like questioning that but kept silent.

'Her... *your* solicitor, Mr Henry.'

Yes now I remembered him, but why would he be here? Longhorn continued. 'Doctor Cecil Dunstable of the London Institute, and his assistant Doctor Wells.'

I nodded my head politely as each name was called. Longhorn looked towards the window at the two men standing there.

A SEA OF DEAD

'Detective Harry Smith, and Mr Bernard Slop.' The man from the restaurant, the one in the brown suit, I ignored both.

'What's this all about?' I asked Longhorn. Longhorn remained silent, unable it seemed to think of anything to say to me, he even looked a little embarrassed.

'Mr Sherman.' It was Mary's solicitor Mr Henry who spoke, rising from his chair and placing his hands neatly into his trouser pockets. 'I was called by your wife.' He turned to face her; I wanted to inform him I did know who she was.

'She has become very worried about your health, and more so your behaviour as of late.'

'I am fine,' I said looking at her. 'The doctor here has done a fine job.' I looked at Longhorn who seemed unable to hold my stare. 'I do not understand her concern.'

'Mrs Sherman has felt for some weeks the improvement in your health has somewhat stagnated, and she has felt troubled by your unwillingness to want to leave these premises.'

I smiled at him and glanced up towards the clock, it had just gone half past nine.

'Surely that's up to Doctor Longhorn to assess, not my wife, unless I'm mistaken, she is not medically trained to make those suppositions.' I looked at Longhorn who sat tapping his pen on a book.

A SEA OF DEAD

'Well... well...' He looked suddenly nervous. 'I must say after showing immense improvement in the early weeks here, the captain's progress *has* slowed down somewhat.'

I looked at him with astonishment, unable to comprehend what he was saying, but then I glanced across to Mary and all began to come clear.

'I see,' I said now looking directly at her. 'Father has got the cheque book out I see.'

She looked directly back up at me. 'That has nothing to do with this.' Like Longhorn she could not hold my stare.

'Well has he made a contribution to funds doctor?'

'Mr Rawlins has always been a generous benefactor, without people like him we could not continue with our work. But that has no bearing on what we are here today to discuss.'

'No... Are you certain doctor?' I asked.

'I am.'

From behind me a man cleared his throat; along with the rest of the room, I turned to look at him. It was Doctor Cecil Dunstable from the clinic which I had forgotten the name of. He had the thumb of each hand inside the breast pockets of his waistcoat, a heavy gold chain linked to a buttonhole hung between then disappeared into a pocket further down, presumably with an expensive watch at the end.

'May I say...' He removed his hands and clasped them behind his back. 'I think Doctor Longhorn's work here is staggering, and let me take my hat off to him.' He looked at Longhorn and smiled, Longhorn glowed at the praise heaped upon him.

He has done wonders repairing broken bodies; no man had done more to help in this war. I myself specialise in the healing of the mind.'

'What in heaven's name are you saying?' I was beginning to lose patience.

'Captain Sherman *if* I may continue...' He had one of those soft irritating voices that crept under your skin. 'We can see the captain's wounds.'
I turned my face away.

'Life-changing injuries that affect the body yet do far more damage to the mind, and they remain long after the scars heal themselves. Just because we cannot physically see these wounds, does not mean they are not there and these are far more damaging than the victims other abrasions.'

I laughed out loud; I could not contain myself any longer.

'Is daddy paying for your research as well doctor?' I asked.

'That is irrelevant sir,' he replied.

'So he is.'

'David can't you listen for once? People are trying to help you.' Mary spoke from her chair.

'I do not need help Mary... not from this man at least.' I looked again at the clock it was now just gone quarter to ten; I felt some anxiety enter my body.

A SEA OF DEAD

'Tell me doctor...' It was the policeman Smith who spoke next. 'What do you mean? How does it manifest itself?'

'I am glad you asked,' said Dunstable, who was treating this like a seminar, a platform to speak to an audience. 'Gloom descends on the patient, not wanting to dress or shave, drinking to excess at strange times of the day, and being unable to see what others around them do, including loved ones. Then there is the aggression, whether physical or with the violent use of words.'

'Can someone tell me where this is going?' I interrupted.

'Captain *please*,' said Smith. 'Continue doctor.'

'It seems the captain here has been showing all those signs, he spent three days unable to move from his bedroom, the staff told me how he began to grow a beard, his washing bowl was not used...'

'This is unbelievable!' I laughed out loud. 'That is no proof.'

'Captain Sherman.' It was the policeman again. 'Do you know this gentleman sir?' He pointed to the man standing next to him.

'I vaguely remember him from the restaurant.'

'His name is Bernard Slop, a highly respected businessman, a man held in high esteem, benefactor to our church, and a pillar of our society.'

'All very nice,' I said, 'but what has that to do with me?'

A SEA OF DEAD

'Two evenings ago you threatened to shoot this man.'

'I *what?*'

'Do you deny it sir? Because we have witnesses... *including* your own wife who will verify that.'

'Then people will remember me saying, *if* I had a gun I would shoot him.'

The room stirred.

'You admit it sir?'

'No, I had no gun so how could I shoot him.' I laughed but no one else seemed to.

'But you made the threat sir.'

'In the heat of the...'

'You made the threat sir?'

'Yes... but.'

'Had you been drinking?'

'I had a glass of wine with my meal.'

'Your wife said it was far more than one glass.'

'Okay two glasses, I can drink two glasses of wine and not be drunk for Christ's sake.'

'Doctor Longhorn...' It was Dunstable. 'Would you advise Captain Sherman to drink?'

'As far as I knew he had not drunk since his arrival here.'

'Is that so?'

'So I had some wine!' I looked around the room for support, there was none forthcoming. I looked up at the clock, almost ten.

'If you had been carrying a gun sir...' Smith spoke again.

'But I was not.' I reached for my cigarettes.

'Do you still have your army revolver sir?'
I looked at the ceiling blowing out a cloud of smoke.
'Yes... yes I have.'

'So you might well have had that about your person, and in that case, the threat could become a reality.'

Again I laughed out loud, and even to my own ears I began to sound like a madman.

'This is crazy,' I shouted. 'I am not mad nor am I ill, and I am certainly not in need of a mental doctor... But I would like to be gone from this room gentlemen...' With that I made my way to the door.

'Sir, please do not attempt to leave this room,' said Smith in his *best* policeman's voice.
I stopped and turned around.

'Mr Slop has made a serious complaint, one I take very seriously indeed, but I can also see you have served your country well, and have suffered as a consequence. Mr Slop can also see that, and has no wish to heap more anguish upon your good self.'

Smith walked across the room towards me.

'Mr Slop is a good citizen captain, he is a compassionate man sir, a man who can see suffering and wants to help, and he is not a man who kicks someone when he is down.'

A SEA OF DEAD

I looked across to the feeble looking man, unable to relate the description Smith was giving me, to the man I was looking at.

'I have spoken to Mr Slop, to both the good doctors and your wife, and we have come up with a solution sir, Mr Slop will drop his complaint, if you agree to spend some time at Doctor Dunstable's clinic.'

'You have to be joking... What's going on here? Firstly Mr Slop's complaint is hearsay, and the rest is all madness. You sir...' I looked at Smith. 'Cannot arrest me; not on a complaint.'

I made my way to the door again.

'David.' It was our solicitor who spoke above the noise. 'Your wife is worried about you.'

'So?'

'After speaking to these doctors she feels it would be wise to spend some time at the clinic, she said the children are also worried.'

'Trudy and Lizzy are fine,' I shouted back across the room. 'What in God's name have you been saying to them Mary?'

'Both girls are scared to visit David.'

'That is rubbish.' Full of anger I stormed across the room. 'You lying bitch.'

Mary screamed and placed her hands across her face as if I was about to strike her.

'WHAT ARE YOU DOING?' I shouted.

'GET HIS ARM.' A voice shouted.

Mary screamed again, and the room began to blur.

A SEA OF DEAD

'GET HIS ARM.'

I felt my sleeve being pulled up, I struggled but I felt overwhelmed, and my leg began to hurt. My sleeve button was undone and my arm gripped more tightly.

'Wells... *now.*'

I felt a sharp stinging pain and looked down as the needle was being withdrawn from my skin; Dunstable's assistant looked at me. I looked up at the clock it was ten past ten, then slowly I began falling, I felt my arms and body come suddenly free, now I was in free fall, I looked down and saw just darkness.

༺༻

A mist covered the ground, it was nighttime yet the sky above was red and not black. The stars that were scattered about it looked pink in colour. There was silence, nothing moved except the mist which hovered inches from the ground. I was standing on mud; I looked down at it and stared, while a brown liquid covered my boots as they pressed into the soil. Six-foot-high walls of earth were either side of me, held in place with wood. All around you could sense a feeling of terror.

I felt the need to walk forward; somewhere up ahead was my destiny. The trench seemed to go on and on, and the mud continued to suck at the soles of my boots, as if trying to slow my progress. I realised now that the pain in my leg had vanished, but how could that

A SEA OF DEAD

be? I then touched my jaw, and felt its smoothness under my fingertips; there were no abrasions to the skin, the surface appeared to be untouched.

I saw a couple close together up ahead, and continued towards them. The boy looked up first. He had been talking to a very young girl, both smiled now in my direction.

'Everything alright sir?' The boy stood upright.

'Yes fine,' I replied.

The girl looked up and I recognised her from the farm, I smiled and she returned it.

'She is seeing me off sir,' the boy continued.

'Try not to be sick lad,' I said before moving on.

I continued to walk on; looking up I noticed the sky was now an even deeper red. In the far distance I saw a bright white light. Two people were silhouetted against it ahead; they stood side by side. I walked on until I reached Marlin.

She smiled as I grew ever closer. 'Captain,' she whispered, 'meet Alan.' She turned to face him, and at the same time placed her arm around his waist. Strangely, I did not feel any jealousy, instead I felt pleased for her.

'Pleased to meet you,' I said and we shook hands. Then both kissed right there in front of me, I looked away unable to shoulder the burden of loss.

'When you're ready sir.' The voice came from above me.

I looked up and saw Private Young sitting smoking his poorly made cigarette. I smiled upon seeing him. A

A SEA OF DEAD

wooden ladder rested against the muddy wall, and I began to climb it; I heard Young mumbling. I reached the top and stood next to the sitting solider; the mist had lifted several feet and now I could see what it hid; a sea of bodies as far as the eye could see, one piled upon the other.

'What a waste,' said Young.

'Yes private, such a waste of good people.'

'A sea of dead sir… that's what it is… a sea of dead.'

From below I heard movement and looked down; the boy kissed the farmer's daughter on her cheek and smiled, she returned it and he stepped onto the ladder and began to climb.

'Thanks for this sir,' said Young.

'For what Young?'

'Your whistle sir, we needed your whistle.'

'My whistle?'

The boy reached the top and stood smiling.

'Didn't piss me pants this time sir, or throw up for that matter.' Pleased with himself he smiled, and I saw he was no more than seventeen. 'Good of you to do this sir.' He added still with that boyish grin.

There was movement on the ladder once more and Marlin's Alan came to the top; I looked back down into the trench, where both Marlin and the French girl were embracing.

'Thank you.' Marlin mouthed the words.

'Right sir we are all ready.'

A SEA OF DEAD

'For what Young?' My mind had gone blank.

'To join the dead sir, it's why you're here... the whistle; you must blow the whistle for us to join them.'

I understood; they needed to follow instructions, without orders or someone to instruct, they were powerless to move. They had joined up to fight for their county, not to think, but to be told what to do and when, and to do it without questioning it in any way.

I placed the whistle in my mouth; it seemed to stick between my dry lips.

'Well sir?' said Young as the other two smiled placing their guns over their shoulders.

I blew as hard as I could and at that precise moment felt a droplet of liquid hit me on my cheek, that was followed by another and then another, before the heavens opened up. I looked down; the earth was now like the sky... red. I looked at my hands, they too were crimson in colour, I looked up and saw that it was not rain that fell, but blood, I allowed it to hit my face, then from somewhere inside I felt a roar force its way to my throat, I opened my mouth and began to scream.

THE END

A SEA OF DEAD

If you enjoyed A Sea Of Dead and would like to be kept informed of my new book launches, please subscribe to my mailing list http://AuthorRobertFowler.com/subscribe.

Reviews are always welcome.

Thank you.

About The Author

Robert Fowler was born in June 1954 in Bethnal Green, London, to an English father and an Italian mother.

He left school at fifteen with GCE Maths, English and History. His first job was working in a warehouse that sold plumbing and heating supplies. He still remains in the industry today, running his own company which he started in 1988.

He lives and works in Hertfordshire and is married with one daughter.

Made in the USA
Charleston, SC
25 November 2013